ANGELS OF DEATH

A private investigator uncovers more than he bargained for when he looks into the apparent suicide of an accountant ... what secrets are hiding inside the sinister house on the coast of Ireland that Martin O'Connell has inherited from his eccentric uncle ... ? A hitherto unknown path appears in the remote Appalachians, leading Harvey Peterson deep into the forest — and a fateful encounter ... And an Indian prince invites an eclectic group of guests to his palace to view his unique menagerie — with unintended consequences ... Four tales of mystery and murder.

EDMUND GLASBY

---◆---

ANGELS
OF DEATH

Complete and Unabridged

LINFORD
Leicester

First published in Great Britain

First Linford Edition
published 2017

Copyright © 2015 by Edmund Glasby

*A catalogue record for this book is available
from the British Library.*

ISBN 978–1–4448–3167–2

Published by
F. A. Thorpe (Publishing)
Anstey, Leicestershire

Set by Words & Graphics Ltd.
Anstey, Leicestershire
Printed and bound in Great Britain by
T. J. International Ltd., Padstow, Cornwall

This book is printed on acid-free paper

Contents.

Angels of Death

*Their music was far
from heavenly.*

April 1945

The sounds continued to beat at the composer's ears, building with terrible intensity to the finale that he knew was close at hand. The screams and sobs, the animalistic outpourings of grief and fear from the doomed people in the room below, were being drawn through him and into the electronic monster to which he had been wired up. He prayed with all his might that he would die before the machine was able to capture the distilled pain and despair. If his heart gave way, it would stop the psychic transfer onto the recording device, and this dreadful use of his gifts would be over. Ever since he had been captured, he had feared death, but now he wanted nothing more than for his torment to end so that others might be saved. Tears, mingled with sweat, ran down his face as the sounds reached a *crescendo — and then abruptly cut off in a mental death cry that echoed through his mind and broke the flimsy barrier of his sanity.*

The recording equipment continued for a few more seconds before a black-gloved hand reached out and turned it off. The owner of the hand regarded the shrieking wreck of a man with some satisfaction before ordering his execution. He had what he needed, although it would take a while to perfect. The priority now was to get out of the country and keep a low profile. A smile creased his lip as an idea came to him.

November 1978

Bespectacled, forty-seven-year-old private investigator John Salford got out of his car, retrieved his briefcase from the back seat, locked up, and stood for a few seconds appraising the large detached red-brick house before him.

Clearly he was in the wrong business, he reflected; for such a property, especially in an area like this, did not come

4

cheaply. Shivering a little in the cold morning air, he lit a cigarette and took several much-needed puffs before throwing it to the pavement and stubbing it out under the heel of a highly polished shoe. Straightening his tie, he then pushed open the garden gate and walked along the short stretch of flower-bordered drive, noticing the figure at the downstairs window. The front door was opened a moment later by his prospective client, the recently widowed Mrs Sally Parker.

'Hello,' she said. 'I take it you're Mr Salford.'

'Yes, that's me.'

'Please, come in.'

'Thank you.' Salford entered the house. 'It's a nice place you've got here, Mrs Parker. Very nice.' Noticing the slightly haggard look in the late-middle-aged woman's face and the weariness behind her eyes, he could see that the sudden death of her husband had, naturally enough, hit her hard. 'May I first offer you my deepest condolences. Obviously I didn't know your husband, but from what little I've been able to find out so far he was clearly a well-liked individual. I'm sure he'll be sadly missed.'

'He will indeed.' Sally gave a half-hearted smile.

Fully aware that this would have to be handled delicately, yet knowing that sometimes the best thing was to get down to business, Salford reached into an inner suit pocket and removed an envelope which he handed over. 'This is just a standard contract letter. It contains all the information relating to my fees, expenditures, what I can and can't do, and all the other admin stuff.'

'Very well. I'll read it later.' Sally placed the letter on a small stand. 'Shall we go into the lounge? And would you like a drink? Tea? Coffee?'

Salford shook his head. 'Not for me, thank you.'

Sally led the way into the well-furnished room. She had obviously prepared things for this meeting, for two chairs and a desk had been set up at one end, atop which rested several large binders and two box-files.

'You said on the phone that your

husband Michael was an accountant,' said Salford. He sat down and removed a pen and a small black notebook from the same pocket from which he had extracted the contract letter.

'That's correct.' Sally sighed and collected her thoughts. There was no doubt it was going to be hard dredging through Michael's documents in such detail. 'He worked in the City at the private accountancy firm Harrington's for twenty years before deciding to go freelance. Although I never met any of his clients, Michael called them his 'luvvies'. They comprised in the main retired actors, over-the-hill performers and the like. Eccentrics mostly. The kind of people who may have been famous forty years ago but are now largely forgotten. You see, Michael's grandfather had been a turn-of-the-century entertainer — a magician, I believe. So he'd always had an interest in things like that, old variety acts and such. Anyway, he'd obviously found a niche for himself, dealing with such people.'

'Interesting.' Salford sat back in his

chair, interlacing his nicotine-stained fingers. 'Now, I hope you don't mind me speaking candidly, Mrs Parker, but I suppose we'd better try and establish just why it is that you think your husband did not . . . well, take his own life.'

Having done some research in order to find out the 'back story', he had read that Michael had been seen by several witnesses clutching his head before purposefully throwing himself in front of a London bus. A post-mortem examination had ruled out anything like a seizure or drugs, which only left suicide. Case closed.

Sally choked back a tear. 'My husband had absolutely no reason to kill himself. We were happily married. As you can see, we have a lovely house. He had just received a glowing endorsement from the highly regarded Board of Independent Accountants. Everything was going so well . . . And then I came home from a brief stay at my sister's to find the police here. It just doesn't make any sense.'

'Is there any history of mental problems in the family? Michael's family, that is.'

'None that I'm aware of. Of course, his parents have been dead a long time now.'

'No . . . suicide note?'

'Nothing. Nothing whatsoever. Had Michael left some form of explanation, I might be able to come to terms with his death; but as it is, I'm in limbo. I'm haunted, not knowing if it's something I could have prevented. I feel guilty in so many ways, wondering if there's more I could have done.'

Salford was beginning to get out of his depth. He knew how to track down missing people, and he could muddle his way through the ins and outs of tax evasion, but he had never had reason to console a grieving widow before. 'I take it you're getting some help in this matter, friends you can talk to?'

Sally seemed to ignore his question. She picked up one of the heavy account ledgers. 'I knew everything about his home life and there was nothing wrong there. That only leaves his work. He never mentioned any problems, but there must be an explanation contained in here somewhere. There has to be.' She opened

9

a page at random.

Unsure as to how much good it would do, but coming to the realisation that he had to do something, Salford rose from his chair and walked around the desk so that he could look over the woman's shoulder. On the open page was a meticulously ordered list of dates, names and figures, all contained within neat margins. Sally turned a page, revealing more of the same. The ledger was filled with invoices, expenditure sums, amounts, and financial facts that Salford knew would take hours, if not days, to sift through.

'Clearly your husband was very detailed in his work.'

'I want you to go through all of this. I can pay you well — more than your normal rate, whatever that is.'

Salford winced. It was not so much the prospect of having to face such a time-consuming task, but what he considered to be the likely futility of it.

'Mrs Parker.' He removed his glasses and gave his eyes a quick rub before putting them back on. 'Forgive me for speaking bluntly, but don't you think you're searching for explanations that may not exist? I mean, tragic as your husband's death undoubtedly was, I fail to see how it can be attributed to anything *but* suicide. As a professional, the last thing I want to do, especially at a time like this, is to prolong your pain. I know this can't be an easy time for you, and you don't need the likes of me cashing in on your suffering.'

'I believe Michael was murdered.' Sally closed the thick ledger. 'There! I've said it.'

'How?' Salford asked incredulously. 'The police — '

'Yes, yes. I know the police think it was suicide. But deep down in my heart, I can't accept it. Something or someone drove him to kill himself.'

Technically that was still suicide, Salford thought, but he understood what she meant. If someone intentionally drove Parker to take his own life, then surely they were morally, if not legally, culpable. He was unsure where the law stood on this, but he nodded, mentally resigning himself to accepting the case. He had to at least attempt to bring some measure of closure to the poor woman. And, at the end of the day, he would be getting paid for it.

He reached down and picked up one of the leather-bound ledgers. 'Well . . . I'll look into these accounts for any inconsistences if you want, but please don't get your hopes up.'

★   ★   ★

After stubbing out his tenth cigarette of the evening, Salford paced over to his drinks cabinet and poured himself another whisky. Glass in hand, he stared down at the account files he had spent the last four hours sifting through. It had proven hard, eye-straining, confusing work, and his brain was a chaotic jumble of fiscal workings. His initial hope of finding things fairly straightforward had dissipated after the first half hour as the computations and the mode of recording had become increasingly difficult to follow.

A cursory look through the box-files

revealed that one contained countless unsorted papers: letters, yellowed newspaper cuttings, receipts, several old black and white photographs, and even a copy of the late Michael Parker's last will and testament. The other was crammed with articles and magazines, programmes and brochures, flyers and bulletins, all detailing the weird and wonderful lives and times of the deceased's so-called 'luvvies'.

Salford stood, debating whether he should call it a night and resume his task in the morning or try and get another few hours of work in. Draining his whisky in one gulp, he resumed his seat, checked his watch, lit another cigarette, and decided to work until midnight. As the minutes ticked by, he found himself ruminating on the fact that during the other cases he had worked on, it was usually the paucity of documentation which held him back; while this time, however, there seemed to be too much. It was the classic case of a needle in a haystack, and there was no certainty that there even was a needle to be found.

Methodically and meticulously, Salford

had checked each page of the ledgers as they had been compiled, going through them in chronological order from earliest to most recent. They presented to him a highly accurate picture of the volatile, ever-changing financial fluctuations of Parker's clients. Most were securely within the boundaries of what most people would term extremely well-off, their portfolios extending into six- and even seven-figure values. The finances of one or two had obviously not fared quite as well, however; and there were several instances where scribbled, indecipherable markings in red ink, which appeared to have been documented in some form of code or shorthand, possibly highlighted this.

Going purely on the volume of red ink written alongside a pair of individuals who were referred to simply as O & M, Salford decided to try and concentrate on these two, reasoning that it was as good a place as any to begin. Now that he had finally ascertained a starting place, his spirits lifted somewhat. If there was anything to this investigation, then at least he had something, no matter how tentative, to go on. Now that he had singled out this pair, he began to note their conspicuous recurrence.

It had now gone midnight. Like a bloodhound with a scent, Salford delved deeper, purposefully seeking out anything pertaining to the mysterious O & M. The fact that Parker had always referred to them in such a manner, consistently using the old-fashioned ampersand whilst freely using the word 'and' for all others, was in itself slightly unusual. And, although he was unable to comprehend their full relevance, the sheer preponderance of comments ascribed to their financial status suggested to him that the deceased accountant had become increasingly concerned about something or other.

Was it all just about money? Salford removed his spectacles and nibbled thoughtfully at one of the arms. Surely to God there was nothing here that could drive a man of sound mind and body to suicide?

Putting his spectacles back on, Salford sat up and stretched his arms out.

Glancing at his wristwatch, he was surprised to see that it had just gone one o'clock. He lit himself another cigarette and turned his attention to the amassed documentation and other bits and pieces in one of the box-files. Assuming correctly that there was no real order to it, he tipped the contents onto his desk and began rifling through. Much of it was personal effects: an old driving licence, a marriage certificate, a school achievement for something or other, National Service papers and —

Salford's eyes were drawn to a small newspaper cutting. It was typed in French, of which he could read little, and was over twenty years old, dated August 11th 1955. One line stood out: *Mademoiselle Ophelia & Mademoiselle Margaret.*

Were these O & M? If so, then Salford knew of them. Lady Ophelia and Dame Margaret, as they were now known, were the stage personae of a rather clapped-out drag act still treading the boards in some of the less prestigious seaside playhouses: a poor man's Hinge and Bracket by all accounts, whose act was often laced with a smattering of 'seaside postcard' innuendo. He seemed to recall they had once featured in a television advertisement for some lesser-known brand of sherry or something similar, giggling like overgrown schoolgirls as they quaffed and cavorted. They had to be in their late fifties or early sixties by now. Salford scribbled something down in his notebook and decided it was now time for bed.

★   ★   ★

Two long days of searching through Parker's files had yielded nothing of note except for the mystery of the red annotations which Salford was certain had been written in some kind of code. With only this to go on, he decided to talk to each of those clients about whom there were red notes. If he were honest with himself, he was also becoming more than a little curious about Lady Ophelia and Dame Margaret, so he had decided to start with them.

Despite a fairly intensive search, he had

been unable to find out the real names of the two cross-dressing entertainers, which perplexed him. However, their address, just outside London, had been more forthcoming, contained as it was in some correspondence between them and Parker. As he turned into the private drive, he mentally tried to work out how he would initiate his inquiry.

There was little doubt in his mind, and indeed in the minds of those who were aware of them, that they were a homosexual couple: eccentrics and recluses who, aside from their flamboyantly camp and inimitably over-the-top performances, now shunned all contact with others. Salford had to assume that they had been informed of their accountant's death. If not, it would be up to him to break the bad news.

The fact that the duo did not appear to have an agent was something that also intrigued him. Admittedly, they were getting a bit past it, but he still thought they would have had some form of representation. The situation was not unprecedented, but it was unusual.

After he had parked, Salford locked his

car up and made his way to the main entrance. It was a substantial house, set in grounds that may have been neatly kept in the past but were now running to seed. Few places looked their best in winter, but it was clear that nothing had been done to keep the gardens in good condition for a long time. The gravel surrounding the building was patchy and weed-filled — a sure sign of years of neglect. From its steeply pitched gables to the ornate iron conservatory, now missing several panes of glass, it must have been a perfect example of a grand Victorian house.

Salford had to supress a shiver. Places like this always reminded him of ghost stories. Looking up at the small windows on the top floor, he could imagine a despairing face looking out, silently screaming for help.

He stopped at the door. On his right was an old-fashioned bell pull, and he was just about to reach for it when he heard a series of bolts being drawn back. The door opened.

The sight that greeted the private

investigator was as strange as it was surprising. He had never expected one of the middle-aged thespians to answer the door, dressed and made up in the Edwardian fashion they were known for, complete with beauty spot, a peacock feather in what was surely his wig, a long jade-green dress, gloves, stylised cameo brooch, pearl necklace, and drooping earrings. Yet such was the case.

'Yes, what is it?' The man's voice was nasal, high-pitched and snobbish; condescending to the point of insulting. From the smell of it, he had doused himself in lavender.

Salford hesitated, unsure how to proceed. He had prepared himself for several eventualities but this had not been one of them. 'Pardon me for asking, but are you . . . Lady Ophelia or Dame Margaret?'

'As you ask, I am Dame Margaret.'

Things were bordering on the surreal for Salford. Despite his reluctance, he found himself scrutinising the drag queen, his face creasing with disapproval the more he saw. It was like something he had last seen at a pantomime when he had been a child: ghastly, yet at the same time strangely fascinating. It was one thing seeing individuals like this on the stage, but to be confronted by one on the doorstep to his home was quite another. Unless a performance was imminent — which, given the early hour of the day, Salford doubted — such things were far from normal. He opened his mouth to speak but no words came out.

'Margaret, darling. Have we a visitor?' called out a mellifluous voice from within the hallway. A moment later another made-up man, resplendent in a rich scarlet dress, choker, gloves and tiara stepped into view. Reaching into his handbag, he removed a monocle which was then deftly fastened to his right eye. With a giggle, he stepped unnervingly closer. 'Well, let's have a look. My, such a fine specimen of manhood.'

'I agree, Ophelia. Perhaps we ought to have him stuffed,' quipped Margaret in sudden good humour. 'You know how good I am at taxidermy. I daresay he'd

21

make an excellent contribution to my collection.'

Ophelia smiled. 'But think of the mess, dear. We no longer have any servants to do the tidying.'

Salford raised his arms. 'Look, I fully get your banter or whatever the hell it is you guys are — '

'Guys?' The two drag queens turned to each other in shared confusion before turning their gazes on Salford.

'Am I right in thinking that you are of the opinion that we are . . . *men?*' asked Margaret. Undoubtedly offended, he drew in his cheeks so that it looked as though he was sucking on a lemon.

'Please, you can drop the act. Save it for your shows.' Salford was growing uncomfortable and impatient. There was little hope in getting much from these two weirdoes if they were to persist with their bizarreness. 'I'm here to inform you that your accountant, Michael Parker, is dead.'

'What a . . . tragedy,' commented Margaret.

'Yes indeed.' With actions that were as

blatantly insincere and disrespectful as they were exaggerated, Ophelia withdrew a silk handkerchief from his handbag and began to wipe false tears from his cheeks.

'Now see what you've done.' Margaret put a comforting arm around his other half. 'There, there, dear.' He fixed the private investigator with a scathing stare. 'Look! You've gone and given her the sniffles. I'll ask you to leave and take your bad news elsewhere. You're not welcome here. Begone, and bother us no more!'

Not for the first time in his life, Salford found the door slammed in his face.

★   ★   ★

After his failure to get any information from Ophelia and Margaret, Salford meticulously checked through the other clients about whom Parker had left cryptic notes. All had been extremely helpful and genuinely saddened to hear of their accountant's death, in stark contrast to the reaction of the two he had met the day before.

An elderly actress, whom Salford

vaguely remembered seeing on screen, had told him that they would all be hard put to find another accountant who had such a good grasp of show business. She had also given him a clue about Parker's notes. Apparently she received a regular payment from an ex-lover who, though he was still fond of her, did not want their history to become public. When she had mentioned the name of a prominent married politician, Salford pricked up his ears. What if the notes were all to do with secrets that Parker had either been told in confidence, or had worked out for himself? If so, then Ophelia and Margaret might have a lot to hide and possibly a lot to lose.

Salford knew he had to decipher Parker's code, and decided that the person most likely to know how to solve this conundrum was Sally Parker. She agreed to meet him in a quiet coffee shop near to his office that he liked to use to relax nervous clients.

'You mentioned on the phone that you were planning to pay a visit to some of Michael's 'luvvies'. Do you have any news for me?' Sally asked, eager to hear of any developments.

Salford took a sip from his steaming coffee cup before returning it to the table. 'Not news as such, but the visits have thrown up a few questions that I hope you can help me with. Some of the entries in your husband's records have coded writing beside them. It may be important that we decipher them, and I wondered if you know how to read them.'

'Those scribbles?' Sally asked in surprise. 'No idea, I'm afraid. Aren't they just to do with calculations?'

'The first few seem to have been, but as I went further into the records they changed. The later notes look far more like coded writing. Let me show you.'

Salford removed a few photographs he had taken of the pages in question. 'See this one? These are all letters, but I can't make head or tail of them.'

Sally took the photographs. 'I see what you mean. It doesn't look like shorthand. I was a secretary before I married and I would recognise that.' She stared at the photographs for a few moments before shaking her head. 'I'm sorry, but this doesn't mean anything to me. Michael often talked about his clients and he loved to tell me some of their anecdotes, but he never discussed their finances with me. Do you think this might be important?'

'It could be. I'm beginning to think that your husband knew more about his clients than some of them would have wanted. I imagine that discretion is important in his line of work?'

'Of course! He would have needed to know all about their financial affairs to do his job, and people don't generally want those facts to be broadcast.'

Salford lit a cigarette. 'Yes, but I was thinking more on the lines of embarrassing secrets or incriminating behaviour. Would he have come across anything of that nature?'

'Well, I think there were a few times when he had to ask directly for an explanation of money coming in or going out that he could not account for. Now that you mention it, there *was* something. Something that he got worked up about.'

Behind his spectacles, Salford's eyes narrowed. 'What was it?'

'It would have been about two years ago, when he took on some new clients. He spent at least a week working through the files from a previous accountant and he was very distracted, worried almost. Then it suddenly got better and he was back to normal. I haven't thought about it since.'

'Can you remember who the clients were?' Salford asked eagerly.

'Yes, I'm pretty sure it was the musical comedy act, Ophelia and Margaret.'

Salford tensed. 'How sure, exactly?'

Sally thought for a moment and then nodded her head. 'It was definitely them. He said they were the most colourful characters he had ever met. Personally, I've always thought them a little weird; creepy almost. Still, I'd be most surprised if they've got anything to do with Michael's death.'

'Have you ever met them?'

'No, but I've heard a bit about them and I saw them on television once or twice. I have a feeling they once starred alongside Morecambe and Wise. Or was it Benny Hill?'

'Acting on a hunch, I went out to see them yesterday. I've met some strange people in my line of work, but there's something about those two that sets my teeth on edge.' Salford reached into his jacket pocket and removed his notebook. 'There are a few questions I'd like to ask you. Firstly, how's your French?'

'Reasonable . . . I suppose. Why?'

'As you know, your husband kept many articles and notes on his clients.' Salford opened his notebook and took out the small newspaper cutting which had steered him towards the two drag queens. He handed it over. 'I'm okay with German, but I never got the hang of French. Can you read this?'

Sally took the cutting and quickly read it to herself, her eyebrows rising in surprise. 'Okay. It reads as follows: During a performance by Mademoiselle Ophelia and Mademoiselle Margaret a man barged onto the stage, shouting wildly, and seemed about to attack the stars. Security men ran to stop him, but he produced a gun and shot himself in the head. The authorities are currently investigating, but no one apart from the gunman was hurt. This comes two weeks after the tragic suicide of the Mademoiselles' manager, Monsieur Guillaume Baschel.'

She looked up from the cutting and there was a spark in her eyes. 'Two suicides!'

'It's certainly an interesting coincidence.' Salford tried to sound cautious and level-headed, but he too felt a building hope that this could be a real lead.

'You need to go back and get some answers from them,' Sally insisted.

'I will, but I want to do some more checking first. There may be more about the incident in Paris, and there must be people who can dish the dirt on them. Show business is supposed to be gossipy. Hell, I haven't even been able to find out their real names yet.'

The private investigator drained his cup and asked for the bill. 'Check at home to see if there are any other papers that might relate to all this,' he said to Sally.

'Yes. If I find anything, I'll call you.' She rose to leave and then sat down again abruptly. 'I've just thought! You should ask Ernest Harrington about Michael's notes. He was Michael's employer for twenty years and taught him most of what he knew.'

'Good thinking! I'll get straight on to it,' Salford agreed. He felt a renewed vigour, as at last there was something to grab hold of in this case. He would put his friend, Gerry Lomas, onto searching old newspapers for anything about Ophelia and Margaret. Lomas worked as a librarian and was always glad of a supplement to his income, particularly if he could do his research when the library was not busy. His own time would be better spent at Harrington's.

*   *   *

'Oh, yes. I recognise these.' Ernest Harrington ran his finger down the page of the ledger that Salford had handed him. He was a thin, balding man who was fast approaching retirement age.

'Can you decipher them?' Salford asked.

'Of course! It's my own invention. Sort of a cross between shorthand and anagrams. Poor Michael picked it up very quickly. I use it when I need to make a note of something delicate that I would not want to become common knowledge but don't want to forget.'

'So what do they say?' Salford tried to summon his patience but he was dying to know.

'Let's see. What have we got here?' Like an Egyptologist poring over a sheet of ancient papyrus, Harrington began to translate the cryptic notes. ''South American funds. Illegal brokers, check for implications. Payments to F. Moreau draining account. Clients refuse to reveal details.' Etcetera. Hmm . . . interesting stuff,' he commented, and moved on to the next section of red notes.

'This is from a few weeks later. More of the same. 'Chilean investments doing better than expected.' Here Michael writes that the funds have been disposed of and payments ceased. What's this? 'O and M explained that F. Moreau had been a penniless relative whose medical bills they had paid, but he had unfortunately died.''

Salford was disappointed. So far there was little to help with his case. He was about to thank Harrington for his time when the elderly accountant made a sudden exclamation and peered more closely at the page he was examining.

'This is the last entry and the last section of annotation.' Harrington pointed to the text he was studying. 'Michael writes that there was a large payment from Paraguay in October, far larger than any other the two had received before. It was from the same source as the ones he was concerned about when he took on their accounts.'

'Sorry, I'm confused. I don't quite understand the problem with investing in South American businesses,' Salford confessed.

'Oh, mostly it's fine, and there are some very good opportunities for long-term investors. But there have been warnings of quite a high level of criminal activity, drug cartels and the like. I always advise my clients to be very vigilant about any investments from that area in case there's a connection. I'm sure Michael did the same, and I'm not at all surprised that he flagged up this payment and was going to ask them about it.' Harrington returned his attention to the page. 'It says: 'Have arranged meeting with O and M. Eleven thirty, November First.''

'But that was the day before he died!'

Harrington looked at Salford with dawning horror. 'Do you mean to say that you suspect that O and M, whoever they are, had a hand in his death? I thought he'd committed suicide. Leapt in front of a bus or something.'

'Maybe, maybe not. It's too early to jump to conclusions. Tell me, if Parker found evidence of a client taking part in illegal activities, and not for the first time, do you think he would have informed the police?'

'If he had real evidence, I'm certain of it,' Harrington answered with conviction. 'He was absolutely straight.'

★   ★   ★

It was proving to be an eventful day. After his interview with Harrington, Salford called on Sally to check if her husband had indeed visited Ophelia and Margaret on the day before his death. As she had been at her sister's at the time in question, however, she could not confirm it either way. But she did have news of her own. She had shown him the latest edition of the *Radio Times* because there was an article about the forthcoming Royal Variety Performance. And, much to his surprise, near the end of the list of acts were Lady Ophelia and Dame Margaret. How exactly they had managed that was beyond him. He knew the Royal Variety Performance was a rather eclectic mix, but even so . . .

Leaving to do some research of his own, Salford called Lomas and felt a certain grim satisfaction at the librarian's discoveries. The records showed that the two performers had come to England from France in the early sixties and had left a mysterious trail of death in their wake. It appeared that at least seven people who had some connection with them had taken their own lives: three stage managers, a theatre critic, a make-up artist, a cleaning lady, and a journalist. Strange as the deaths had been, there did not seem to have been any suspicion on the police's behalf that the two drag artists were involved, and the incidences had happened far enough apart that they did not pursue this.

Salford felt as if the pieces of the puzzle were finally falling into place, though he still had no idea how the deaths had been effected. Was it all just coincidence, or could the pair have used some kind of hypnosis to plant a death wish in their victims' minds? In Parker's case, could one of them have actually pushed him under the bus and just not been noticed by the witnesses? Were they guilty or innocent?

Of one thing Salford was certain: they were dangerous to know, for death surrounded them. He knew the facts did not add up, and there was definitely something to be discovered. He had debated whether to go to the police but felt that he simply did not have enough to go on yet. As it was, he did not even know if Parker had in fact gone to see his two clients as he had planned. They could always deny it anyway. What he needed was some hard evidence.

Sitting in his office, Salford wondered whether or not he should approach the pair directly. Given the reception he had got last time, maybe not. What he really wanted was to take a look inside their house and see if there were any skeletons hiding in the closet amid the sequined ball gowns and cocktail dresses.

Remembering the article in the *Radio Times*, Salford had a sudden inspiration. The show was to be recorded tomorrow and there would surely be rehearsals before then. He telephoned the London Palladium pretending to be an electrician, and ascertained that the main rehearsals were to be held today before the main performance tomorrow, and that all the acts would be there for several hours. The office manager had told him that they did not generally finish until late evening.

Salford's mind was made up. This was his chance.

*   *   *

The early-evening air was bitterly cold, and one or two stars were beginning to show through the breaks in the cloud as Salford emerged from the shadows and scaled the wall which surrounded the foreboding property. Stealthily he dropped to the other side, pleased to see that all was in darkness. Now that he was inside the grounds, everything was suddenly ominous.

In the course of his numerous investigations, he had only once before had reason to resort to breaking and entering. He took out his heavy torch, comforted by its solidity in his hand. In the far distance an owl hooted.

Clinging to what shadows there were, Salford crept towards the house. Warily he made his way around the back of the building. Removing a small jemmy from his coat pocket, he searched for a convenient window, then set about levering it open. Once done, he switched on his torch and shone it inside. Aside from the dancing shadows, there was no movement.

Nerves afire, Salford clambered into the room. It was small and had the appearance of a scullery. Shining his torch around, he saw a vast Belfast sink and racks for dishes to dry on, a large wooden tub and a mangle. Moving through an archway to the kitchen, the feeling of stepping back in time continued. There was a scrubbed wooden table and an old range for cooking on. Not a sign of any modern white goods was visible. More importantly, nothing to confirm his suspicions about the house's owners.

Exiting the kitchen, Salford went through to a wide hallway with several doors opening off it and a fine staircase. The first main room he entered was undoubtedly for entertaining. There were ornate — if slightly faded — sofas, elegant chairs, and a grand piano covered with photographs of Lady Ophelia and Dame Margaret at various stages of their none-too-illustrious careers.

Again, the room was stuck in a time warp. Two large gilt-edged mirrors reflected the torchlight, and every flat surface had valuable-looking ornaments on them. There was even a yellowing newspaper bearing the date 1910 that had been placed on a side table, and countless other little period features that added to the genteel yet decidedly strange ambience. Salford searched the room thoroughly, but to little effect.

The other large downstairs room felt more private. It appeared to be a study, with two identical desks and chairs. A well-stocked drinks cabinet showed a particular fondness for imported beers, port and brandy — clearly not the sherry Ophelia and Margaret were renowned for tippling on stage. There was a filing cabinet that took Salford's attention for a while, but it contained only information about requests for the duo to appear at various venues over the years, and revealed them to be zealous in their pursuit of the highest fee they could command.

Salford noted that there had been a gap

of several years between their last performance and the very recent letter inviting them to perform at the Palladium. This sudden renaissance in their popularity struck him as strange. Leaving the study, he checked the last door on the ground floor but only found a broom cupboard. That puzzled him; in most houses of this era there was a cellar. Returning to the kitchen, he looked more carefully round the room.

Against one wall was a dresser with a few plates and cups on it. There would have been room for many more, and given the excessive nature of the decoration elsewhere, it looked out of place. Examining it more closely, Salford could see that there were concealed hinges on the far side of the dresser. Wriggling his fingers between the wooden back and the wall, he pulled gently, and was not altogether surprised when the dresser swung smoothly out, revealing a door behind it.

There was a light switch behind the concealed panel; and a little further down a modern strip light, incongruous given its environment, was fixed to the sloping ceiling. A short flight of stairs ended at a plain wooden door.

Cautiously Salford crept down. His heart was thumping in his chest, though whether due to fear or excitement he could not tell. Reaching the door, his heart sank upon finding it locked. Fortunately he was fairly adept at lock-picking, and removing a fine set of picks from a back trouser pocket, he set about diligently trying to gain access. At any moment he half-expected one or both of the owners to appear at the top of the stairs — that he would hear a noise and, upon turning, would see some knife-wielding individual imitating Norman Bates from Hitchcock's infamous *Psycho* shower scene framed in the doorway above.

With a click, the lock sprang. Salford put his lock picks away, then gently pushed the door open. The room beyond was fairly small, perhaps twelve feet by eight, and had been closed and hidden for very good reason — for on the wall directly opposite was a photograph of

Adolf Hitler beneath a large flag bearing the swastika of Nazi Germany!

'What the . . . ?' Shaking his head in disbelief, Salford stepped inside. Panning his torch away from the photograph of the Führer, he could see that the room served as both an office and a private shrine dedicated to the Third Reich. There were several large filing cabinets, two chairs, a desk atop which was a typewriter, a pending tray, some books, a stack of papers, and a gilt-framed photograph. The latter showed three men in white jackets reclining in large wicker chairs. The private investigator's eyes widened as he read the lettering in the small white caption at the bottom: *Schutzstaffel K. Werner, J. Mengele und E. von Koenig. Buenos Aires. 1952.*

Mengele. Josef Mengele. The infamous 'Angel of Death' who had presided over the terrible experimentation on countless Auschwitz concentration camp detainees.

Salford's jaw dropped upon realising that the other two men were none other than Ophelia and Margaret! Even through their disguises, and the fact that the photograph was twenty-six years old, it was possible to recognise them. Unlike other prominent Nazi war criminals, they had not gone to ground, altering themselves through plastic surgery and hiding away in the remotest parts of the world, but had rather done the opposite. For over a quarter of a century, they had evaded capture and fooled the world by masquerading themselves behind the personae of two quintessentially English drag queens, rising above suspicion through their very conspicuousness.

Reasonably fluent in German, Salford began skimming through the papers on the desk. Most were letters; private correspondence between Mengele and his two agents. Others made repeated reference to the Thule Society and Heinrich Himmler's quasi-historical Occult Division — the Ahnenerbe. There were also details of not insubstantial payments from South American benefactors — Nazi sympathisers in the main.

In the pending tray was what appeared to be a scientific document. Expertly typed, it consisted mainly of a long list of names, and caught the private investigator's attention as that at the bottom was Michael Parker. Alongside it was a time: 27 hours and 32 minutes. Two other names Salford recognised: Guillaume Baschel and Francois Moreau. Both individuals who had mysteriously committed suicide.

'Well, hello.'

Salford spun round. Standing in the doorway was Ophelia, or rather SS officer Klaus Werner. Dressed and made up as his feminine alter-ego, he took a casual draw from the slender cigarette holder he had clamped between the fingers of his left hand. In his right hand he held a Luger.

'Margaret dear, guess what I've found?' he shouted.

Gulping nervously, Salford raised his hands.

With an insane giggle, the other drag queen scurried down the stairs and looked over his accomplice's shoulder. 'My, my. It's a good job we decided to come back so that I could get a change of costume. I want to look my best in front of the Queen, after all.'

'I . . . I don't understand,' Salford mumbled. Fear gripped him and he knew that, having discovered what he had, the chances of him getting out of here alive were minimal.

'Of course you don't, dear,' said Ophelia. 'And what's more, you never will. You think that the war ended back in 1945 and that your country, along with the USA and the Russians, stamped out Nazism.' He pulled a sorrowful face and shook his head. 'How presumptuous of you, and how utterly wrong you are.'

'But enough, Ophelia. What are we going to do with him?' asked Margaret.

Ophelia took another draw on the slim cigarette holder, then gave an evil smile.

Margaret clearly understood the unspoken implication. 'Oh, surely not? I thought we only reserved that kind of treatment for our fondest guests.'

★ ★ ★

At gunpoint, Salford was ordered to go upstairs. Once in the study, Margaret

45

searched him, tutting with disapproval when he found and confiscated the lock picks and jemmy. Then he was tightly bound to a chair.

Ophelia stood by an old-fashioned gramophone. 'Now then. Time for a little musical interlude, as they say. But first I'd like to tell you a story.

'Back in 1945 a most gifted, though sadly short-lived, Hungarian composer called Zsiga Zsoldos helped Margaret and me in creating a truly amazing musical score. We had always had a deep fascination with music, sound in particular, and its potential use as a weapon. Through certain mystical means, which I'm sure wouldn't interest someone of your uncouth disposition in the slightest, we created the perfect weapon.'

Margaret came forward with a record. 'Do you remember, Ophelia dearest, how the little children would cry and beg? 'Uncle Josef, can we hear the pretty song?' they would say. How sweet.' Almost reverently, she put the record on to the antiquated turntable.

'I envy you,' said Ophelia, gazing into

46

Salford's eyes, 'as you're going to get to hear the piece in its entirety. Which, for obvious reasons, is something we never have. We didn't manage to work out just how much of the music one needs to hear for it to be effective, but I'd rather not take any chances. For your information, it was said that Zsoldos was in league with the Devil; that he came from Romany stock — accursed gypsies who could harness the powers of darkness. Whatever the case may be, through our perfection and the choral backing of those who were tortured and exterminated, it has the ability to kill; to drive those who hear it to take their own lives. It took long months of experimentation to perfect, and unfortunately it has to be heard directly from the record, of which only this one exists. Just think how useful it could have been to the Fatherland had we been able to broadcast it.

'Now, normally we just leave it playing as background music whilst 'entertaining' those guests who, like the late Mr Parker, begin to get a little too close for comfort.'

'A suspicious one, that. Methinks we

should have done away with him sooner,' added Margaret as he poured himself a brandy.

'Bastards! You'll never get away with this!' Salford shouted.

'Get away with what?' asked Ophelia.

'Murdering me won't get you any-where. People know I'm here. If they don't hear from me in a few hours' time, this place will be crawling with police, and you two can look forward to life in prison.' It was pure bluff on Salford's part, but he knew he had to try something.

'Really?' Ophelia purred. He nodded to his accomplice and the gramophone was switched on. 'Toodle-pip.' The two Nazi drag queens left the study and closed the door.

A crackling sound came from the gramophone — a sure indicator that the record was old and well-played. Then the music began. At first it was just a lone violin playing a simple tune. It was reminiscent of many folk songs from Eastern Europe or Russia and seemed utterly unremarkable.

Salford found he could not take it seriously. Surely this could not be real? No mere music could do what those two claimed it could. He half-expected them to come back in with a loaded syringe or a spiked drink — something that would actually do the job. But if that were the case, then why had no drug been found in Parker's body? His heart lurched a little.

The music was changing. The violin was joined by other instruments and a quiet background sound that seemed vaguely choral. It was not unpleasant, but Salford began to feel slightly unsettled. It was as if something was nagging at the back of his mind. There were no words that he could make out beneath the orchestral work, but he had the disturbing sensation of someone muttering in his ear. The main melody was slow and melancholic, and if he had not been strapped to a chair by two madmen he would have paid little attention to it. With the knowledge of just who he was dealing with and what he had discovered, however, the effect was becoming hard to ignore.

Sweat beaded on his forehead and trickled down the sides of his face as his fists clenched. He now had no doubt that there was something hellish at work. Try as he might to blot the diabolical music out, even singing a different tune as loudly as he could, the sound wormed its way into his ears, subliminally implanting its message of doom deep within his mind. He imagined black leather-gloved hands kneading his brain like dough.

After a few minutes more, the unholy record came to an end. The door to the study opened.

'Finished?' asked Ophelia. Monocle in eye, he regarded the panting Salford with scientific curiosity. 'That's interesting, Margaret. Look at the difference when they know.'

Margaret sipped from his sherry. 'I wonder how long he'll last?'

'Unfortunately we won't be able to time it accurately, as we have other things to do. Can't keep Her Majesty waiting.' Lovingly, Ophelia stroked the gramophone. He looked at Salford. 'You wouldn't believe how long it's taken us to get this far. No doubt you're wondering how we managed to secure a spot on the Royal Variety Performance. Let's just say the current organiser is a big fan of our work. *All* our work.'

'Is that what this is all about?' Salford blurted out. 'You're going to play this at the Palladium?'

'Not a complete idiot after all,' Margaret said sarcastically. 'Yes, the final demonstration of our talents will be a very public affair, the climax of our act! At least, the beginning will be. However, the world will have to wait roughly twenty-four hours to see the full effects.'

'But if you play this on stage, surely you'll be affected by it too?' said Salford.

'My dear boy! Have you never heard of earplugs?' Ophelia exclaimed. 'We've been practising hard to do our entire routine with them in, and I assure you that no one will notice. And then Dame Margaret and I will gracefully retire and go somewhere nice and hot for a little holiday.'

'South America, no doubt.' Salford ground his teeth in fury.

Ophelia clapped his hands and laughed, a jarringly masculine sound. 'What a splendid suggestion!' He pulled out his Luger. Menace sparkled in his piercing blue eyes.

Margaret looked at his watch. 'I think we should get back to our hotel, dear. We do have a dinner reservation, after all.' He produced a knife from his beaded handbag and slit the ropes holding Salford to the chair. 'Now then. Back downstairs with you, you grotty little man.'

Salford was in two minds about making a move to try and overpower the two murderous drag queens. Swiftly coming to the conclusion that such a course of action would only hasten his death, he reluctantly followed instructions. He was taken downstairs and pushed into the secret room.

'We're not completely without pity,' said Margaret. He threw his knife into a corner of the room. 'I think you may need that before the end. But please, try not to make too much of a mess. From our observations of the many test subjects, I can advise you not to fight against the compulsion. The results seem to be . . . most excruciating.'

'*Auf wiedersehen.*' With a nod, Ophelia slammed the door shut. A key was then turned in the lock.

'Bastards! Nazi bastards!' Salford yelled as he hammered on the door. Realising the futility of his actions, he went over to the photograph of Hitler, removed it from the wall and smashed it on the floor.

★　★　★

Three hours later, Salford had only succeeded in breaking the knife while trying to force open the locked door and had nearly broken his shoulder trying to batter it down.

It was while recovering from the latest attempt that he experienced the first wave of pain. It had taken him by surprise — a brief but intense sensation similar to the migraines he had sometimes had. It was gone almost before he had registered it, but there was a strange feeling in his head that lingered for a few minutes.

Taking stock of the situation, Salford sat at the desk to think. He guessed that the performance the following day would start sometime in the early evening. If that were the case, then he might even be dead before then. He found the piece of paper that had Parker's name on it and looked at the numbers next to it: 27 hours and 32 minutes. Presumably that was how long it had taken between Parker hearing the record and killing himself. Looking through the other names and numbers, the times of death varied between twenty-three and thirty hours. If he lasted to the outer limit, that would give him time to stop the murderers, provided he could get out of this room.

The locked door had so far resisted his attempts to batter it down. Salford considered the possibility of going through the wall or ceiling. From what he could remember of the house, there had been no tell-tale low windows to indicate the existence of another cellar, so presumably outside the walls of the room would be packed earth, almost impossible to get through in the timeframe.

The ceiling, however, offered possibilities. Climbing on to the desk, Salford found it was only about a foot above his head. Using the broken blade, he began chipping away at it.

The first thirty minutes' work revealed that the ceiling was plasterboard suspended from wooden joists with floorboards above. He wiped his forehead with his sleeve. The work was awkward and the constant looking up made him feel dizzy, but he was sure he could crack this, given time. Whether he had enough remained to be seen, but under the circumstances there was no alternative. There were obvious parallels with tunnelling out of Colditz.

It was the longest night of Salford's life, and the most stressful. Many times he felt like he could not go on. The aches in his arms and back were dreadful, and he was experiencing more of the waves of pain, which left him light-headed and depressed. At one point, in the early hours of the morning, he had simply succumbed to exhaustion and curled up on the floor to sleep, the torn-down Nazi flag serving him as a pillow.

When he woke, he got back to work. Gradually, he uncovered the joists and found a gap that would be large enough for him to fit through. Then the floorboards had to be weakened enough to break. This was the hardest part of all, and he pulled the heavy carriage out of the typewriter to employ as a hammer. He almost gave up then. The effects of the record were taking their toll, and he found himself looking speculatively at the knife several times, his eyes and mind regarding the sharp blade with a strange fascination; a longing almost. A swift, deep cut across both wrists, and . . .

There came a sudden image of his father, Salford senior, who had stormed the beaches at Normandy trying to rid the world of scum like Werner and von Koenig. He was damned if he would give up while there was still a chance of defeating them. A fragment of Churchill's rousing 'We shall never surrender' speech entered his head.

Eventually only an inch of carpet remained, and the blunted blade made heavy work of the job. Cutting through the last obstacle, Salford made an escape route. Before leaving his prison, he took the photograph of Mengele, Werner and von Koenig and several incriminating documents that would prove who Ophelia and Margaret really were and what they intended to do.

Checking his wristwatch, Salford saw it was a little after five o'clock in the afternoon. He still had time. A visit to the bathroom served to clean him up a little, and a quick search of the two Nazis' bedrooms turned up a second Luger and a large amount of money in various currencies.

Leaving the money, he took the gun, fully loaded, and left the house, aware that there was a time bomb ticking in his head and that the final countdown was fast approaching.

★   ★   ★

A solution to the problem of how to get into the Palladium had come to Salford as he neared the centre of London, and he pulled up outside a florist's. Armed with the most extravagant bunch of flowers they could make for him, he abandoned his car in a side street near the theatre. The waves of pain in his head were becoming more intense now, and began to be accompanied by feelings of soul-crippling despair. His mind was drowning, the sensations threatening to overcome him completely. Reality blurred.

Stepping off the kerb onto the road proper, Salford was startled by the screech of tyres and the angry blast of a taxi's horn. A window rolled down and an irate taxi driver shouted at him before speeding away. In the distance there was the sound of police sirens.

Avoiding the grand entrance of the theatre, Salford made his way to the stage door in a dingy back alley. Unsurprisingly, there was a doorman, but he was leaning casually against the brick wall and smoking a cigar with every evidence of enjoyment.

'Delivery for Lady Ophelia and Dame Margaret,' Salford said briskly.

'All right,' the man sighed. 'Give them here.'

'Can't do that,' Salford replied firmly, and with a hint of self-importance. 'The boss was very insistent that I ensure the arrangement is properly presented. No offence intended, but you'd probably just shove them in a vase or leave them on a table.'

'True enough, I suppose,' the doorman admitted. He considered the fussy-seeming man before him with his carefully combed hair and air of impatience. He also considered having to abandon his cigar to take the flowers inside, and made up his mind. 'Okay, you can nip in. But don't be long.'

Salford thanked him and slipped inside the theatre. Heart pounding, he checked that the Luger was still obscured by the swaths of tissue paper wrapped around the stems, and set out to find the stage. He should be able to find the murderous pair and shoot them before they had the chance to complete their 'experiment'.

The rabbit warren of corridors was busy with the many performers and their assistants, chattering and laughing as they waited their turn or relaxed, having completed their acts. Trying not to stare at people he had only ever seen on the television, Salford followed directions to the stage, once having to squash himself against the wall to allow a group of glamourous dancers in spectacular feathered costumes to get past. Finally, he saw the wings of the stage up ahead.

A stagehand carrying a clipboard came over. 'Stay back there and keep quiet. Who are you looking for?' he asked.

'I'm to give these to Lady Ophelia and Dame Margaret when they come off stage,' Salford lied. 'When are they due on?'

'That's them out there right now,' the man answered. 'Their set's about ten minutes, so you won't have long to wait. I suggest you go to their dressing room.' He turned and went back to his post.

Salford could hear raucous singing. He looked in horror at the sliver of stage he could see from where he was. Sure enough, there was a sofa and a standard lamp of the kind they had in their drawing room. Moving a little closer, he caught a glimpse of the green silk dress worn by Dame Margaret as he enthusiastically swished around the stage, conducting the audience in an exuberant rendition of 'The Marrow Song'.

'Oh, what a beauty! I've never seen one as big as that before!'

The audience were loving it.

Heart thumping, Salford knew he had only a few minutes. Ophelia and Margaret had said that the record would be part of their finale — the ultimate swansong.

'Oh, what a beauty! It must be two foot long or even more.'

Salford checked his inside pocket. The incriminating photograph of Mengele and his protégés was still there, along with the handwritten letter from him, wishing the two good luck in their glorious endeavour. As long as the police found the envelope, it would put them onto the murderers, even if he failed. And if he succeeded in his assassination attempt, at least people would come to know why he had done it. His priority was to prevent the record from being played, whatever it cost him.

He was doomed anyway, if Ophelia and Margaret were to be believed, and he now knew enough to be convinced of that. How many poor wretches had died in agony to create the diabolical musical score? Grasping his head, he could imagine the terrified eyes; could almost feel the emaciated hands reaching out to grab him, beseeching him for help. Innocents — men, women and children who had been reduced to living skeletons; numbers, not names.

The wave of utter despair hit Salford's mind with dreadful force, setting up a stabbing agony in his head. He only had to take the gun out, put it in his mouth, pull the trigger, and it would all be over.

A roar of laughter from the auditorium broke Salford out of his dark contemplation. He stared blankly at his hand, which had been reaching for the Luger, and then thrust it back into his pocket. He had so little time left! The next wave might be the last. He turned his attention back to the stage.

Margaret was telling a long humorous story about an aspidistra, much to the audience's delight. Ophelia had remained seated at the piano and was watching with a kind of restrained eagerness that turned Salford's stomach.

Then he heard it.

The unobtrusive background music that was accompanying the story. God knew how long the record had been playing while he had been caught in a fugue.

Still clutching the flowers, Salford pushed past the stagehands and rushed onto the stage, behind the two performers. With their earplugs firmly in place, they did not at first notice him, whereas the audience burst into a fresh bout of laughter, obviously believing he was part of the act. Grinning inanely, he put his finger to his lips as if signifying a prank to be played on the two 'ladies'. Then he wrenched the record from the gramophone and shattered it over his raised knee.

Noticing the change in their audience, Ophelia and Margaret turned round, and Salford saw the flash of hatred in their eyes. He pulled the Luger from its hiding place and fired twice at Ophelia where he sat at the piano. Having never fired a gun before in his life, he missed, and the next moment he was felled by a punch from Margaret that knocked a tooth out and sent him sprawling onto the sofa in the centre of the stage.

The drag queen was screaming at him in German, calling him all the names under the sun, hands clamping around his throat while the audience looked on in stunned disbelief.

At the gunshot, two policemen materialised as if by magic. One wrestled the Luger from Salford's unresisting grip while the other struggled with Margaret, who looked ready to tear the private investigator to shreds.

Salford could feel the shroud of pain and despair descending again. He fell back onto the sofa. There was nothing else he could do and no way of knowing if the audience had heard enough to seal their fates. The royal box was empty now, its inhabitants doubtless spirited to safety as soon as the first shot had rung out.

He barely felt the policemen bind his hands and caution him. The sound of those tortured and killed in Auschwitz was taking over all his senses, but he saw Ophelia tear off his wig, stand to attention, give the *sieg heil* Nazi salute and, with an insane fervour, start hammering out the tune to the 'Horst Wessel Lied' on the piano.

'Die Fahne hoch! Die Reihen fest geschlossen!' Gone was Margaret's melodic singing voice as he defiantly bellowed out the Nazi Party anthem. Still singing, he was dragged off.

The sight made Salford start to laugh, but soon there were tears running down his face. The awful black despair was back, and the relentless stabbing in his head was worse than before. The urge to kill himself was immensely powerful now, and resisting it was as difficult as holding his breath continuously. The Luger was beyond his reach, and, handcuffed, with a policeman on either side of him, he had little chance to make a run for it. If only he knew whether the record had been playing long enough to implant its deadly message.

The scene before him was fading, the grandeur of the theatre turning into greys and blacks, with shadowy, writhing figures surrounding him. The pain swelled up to claim his mind and he lurched forward.

'How long had the music been playing?' he shouted to the stunned stagehand in the wings. Strong hands grabbed him and he felt himself being dragged to the side.

'What?' The stagehand stared at him in fear and confusion.

'The record! How long had it been playing?' Salford shouted.

'I . . . I don't know. A few minutes perhaps. I wasn't really paying attention,' the man stammered.

The policeman to Salford's right pulled him sharply away. 'You're coming with us.'

'*But how long?*' Salford's yell tailed off and his face began to twist in pain.

Ignoring the police, he slumped over with his head in his lap. Sickened, he could see dead white faces everywhere. They became clearer as the music in his mind crashed its way through his very being. Denied of the opportunity to take his own life, he felt a searing explosion of pain as blood vessels in his brain finally burst. Blood streamed from his eyes and nose. 'How long . . . ?' he mumbled before collapsing, face-first, to the stage.

The Descendant

He was not the only one who had come to claim an inheritance.

The bespectacled solicitor was tall and thin, old and white-headed. He was sitting so straight and stiff in his chair that he looked more like a statue of stone and plaster than a living being of flesh and blood.

'I'm pleased to meet you, Mr O'Connell. My name is Hayes. This is my colleague, Mr Lowry.' He gestured with a knobbly-fingered hand to his associate — a smaller, younger man with a wide, fleshy face who sat fidgeting with the straps of his black briefcase. 'Do come in and take a seat.'

Martin O'Connell sat down at the desk opposite the two solicitors. Hayes drew himself up still straighter in his chair and looked across at his colleague. Lowry handed him a thin sheaf of important-looking papers, which he rifled through quickly before looking up. 'As you've no doubt been informed, your uncle, Patrick O'Connell, passed away some weeks ago.'

71

'Actually, I only found out when I got your letter two days back,' O'Connell replied brusquely. Prior to being told the news, he had forgotten, completely and utterly, about his one remaining relative, someone about whom he had heard nothing for many years. He had been a genuine recluse, who, for some reason known only to himself, had thought fit to shut himself away from the rest of his fellow men.

'Yes, well, I'm afraid it took some time to track down your whereabouts. Anyway, your uncle's solicitors in Killarney contacted us here at our London offices regarding the will, which left everything to his sole remaining relative — namely, yourself. Altogether, the estate is worth a little over half a million pounds, and consists in the main of the house which stands on the low cliffs overlooking Bantry Bay. From all accounts, it's an old rambling building built during the . . . ' Hayes turned to his colleague. 'But there, I think it better if I leave it to my colleague here to explain, as he has spoken to the solicitors about the place.

He can tell you what you want to know about it far better than I can.'

'The house is situated in its own grounds by the side of the cliff road which runs from Bantry out to Sheep's Head Point,' Lowry explained. 'It's quite a wild, forlorn stretch of coastline, especially at this time of the year. The road is treacherous in places and there have been several fatal accidents in the past. If you decide to visit it, I would strongly suggest you find someone who knows the road to drive you there. As Mr Hayes has pointed out, the house is old. It was built sometime during the early sixteenth century, although very little of the original structure still remains. I believe the north wing dates back to that period, but that's about all. Most of the remainder has been added, bit by bit, during later years.'

'I take it it's still habitable?' asked O'Connell.

'Well . . . ' Lowry paused and glanced uneasily at Hayes. 'It's habitable, yes, just about, but — '

'But what?'

'Mr O'Connell,' began the older solicitor, 'you'll find that most of the villagers in Bantry possess some strange superstitious dread of the place, though I'm quite sure that a level-headed person like yourself will not be put off by such foolish nonsense.'

'You mean to tell me that the place is supposed to be haunted?' O'Connell uttered a short bark of harsh laughter.

'I think I ought to mention here, Mr O'Connell, that your uncle was . . . well, a rather peculiar individual. According to the details which we've been given, it would appear that he was a very secretive man who spent most of his time in the house, shunning all contact with the outside world. According to the rumours, he shut himself away in order to delve into, well, demonology.' Hayes adjusted his glasses on the bridge of his thin, pinched nose.

'Demonology?' O'Connell shifted in his seat. 'Surely there's some mistake. You don't intend to rely on the ramblings of a handful of superstitious villagers, do you? I don't doubt they'd see witchcraft in anything. All this prattling about devils and demons and other such stupid things used to be common amongst the uneducated, but surely it's all died out in this day and age? Why, it's bloody ludicrous!'

'Mr O'Connell. Even your uncle's solicitors have expressed this opinion,' claimed Lowry. 'And I can assure you, they struck me as rational people. Now, whether there's any truth in this or not, I cannot say. However, it's indisputable that those living in the vicinity of your uncle's house possess a genuine fear of the place.'

O'Connell shook his head disparagingly. 'What nonsense. Now I'll admit I know very little about this uncle of mine. Haven't seen him for almost twenty-five years. But I can't believe he was engaged in anything so foolish, so utterly ridiculous, as what you're suggesting. Sounds to me as though these people took offence at the way he ignored them and maligned his character.'

Lowry shrugged his shoulders. 'Perhaps. But that's beside the point. I'm just warning you that you had best be prepared for some animosity if you go there.'

'Well, I'll be sure to take along my sacrificial goats and black robes when I pay a visit,' O'Connell quipped.

Hayes looked uncomfortable. 'There is . . . another story concerning the house.' There was an undercurrent of something sinister in his voice.

'Oh? This just keeps getting better. Now, what's this one about? Don't tell me — at midnight the banshee flies around the house, her mournful screams portending death to all who hear it.' O'Connell leaned forward, his elbows along the sides of his chair. 'I always thought that solicitors were sensible people. People who dealt with facts and logic. It seems to me that you two are just as simple-minded as those folk who think that my uncle was into demonology. So what is this story?'

'I . . . ' Hayes regarded the belligerent man before him for a moment. 'Maybe it would be for the best if you found that out for yourself. I take it you'll be going out there?'

* * *

Hands clenched into tight fists on the steering wheel, O'Connell turned out of Macroom and began the hour-long drive to Bantry. Once he arrived, he would make for the most convenient hotel and put up there for the night. It would be sheer stupidity to go on to the house, as it was already getting dark. In spite of himself, he shuddered slightly at the thought.

In vain, he tried to tell himself that this was his only reason for not going straight there, though deep down he knew very clearly that he was being a coward and a fool. In spite of his scepticism, he had not been able to prevent himself from brooding a little over the things that he had been told a week earlier in London.

A heavy rain began to fall as he made his way along the road, the dark, forested humps of the Shehy Mountains looming to his left and right. The headlights picked out the wet, shining surface of the road as the windscreen wiper flicked relentlessly back and forth.

Alone in his car as he wended his way westward to the coast, O'Connell couldn't help but think that perhaps something was already waiting for him with a grim patience, lurking in the house now, knowing he was coming, preparing for his arrival. A sick feeling of impending disaster began to take hold of him. For a terrible moment he dared not look in the rear-view mirror for fear that he would see something — something ghastly and inhuman either sitting in the back seat or flying behind him, readying itself to land on the car.

Breathing deeply, he tried to steel himself and force calmness into his mind. Somehow he realised that his thoughts had become all tangled up inside his brain. He carefully considered all of the events that had led up to his being there, driving through the late-evening murk towards Bantry.

Was there any truth in the speculation that his uncle had delved into demonology? And what of this mysterious other story regarding the house? Why had Hayes and Lowry persisted in hinting at such things? Had they an unscrupulous ulterior motive?

O'Connell swore angrily. First thing in the morning, he would drive up to Killarney and question the solicitors based there, from whom he hoped he would get a clearer picture.

* * *

The rain had almost stopped by the time he drove into Bantry. There was a weathered sign at the side of the road, almost hidden by the huddled shapes of rearing bushes and dark trees. It creaked ominously in the sighing wind. He stopped the car and climbed out, his feet slipping a little on the wet kerb. The black lettering was badly faded, but he finally managed to make it out: 'The Bay Hotel'.

Far ahead and a little to one side, beyond the outline of Whiddy Island, O'Connell could make out the dark and tenebrous form of the headland sweeping around towards the Caha Mountains. He shivered as he looked in the opposite direction to where the land protruded out towards the Atlantic Ocean. For there, silhouetted against the darkening sky, he caught a vague glimpse of something huge and oddly sinister that set his heart racing in his chest, though he didn't quite know why. Some hidden instinct seemed to tell him that this was his uncle's mansion. It was a grim, forbidding structure. Sometime tomorrow he would be inside that supposedly cursed building.

A thin, watery moon was trying its best to shine through the racing clouds. Thick, boiling clouds that seemed to be always running away from some black storm just below the horizon.

O'Connell was startled as a whirl of dried leaves whispered and danced insanely on the smooth boards of the hotel's porch. Others rustled among the dead branches of the trees and bushes, muttering and crackling as though talking to each other in a dead, dried-up language of their own. And above everything else, there was the constant booming of the tide.

There was something about this place that he didn't like. Something horrible and menacing, hidden just below the surface of things. Something that he knew instinctively wouldn't be there in the daylight. But at night . . .

With an effort, he suppressed the dull murmuring of fear that began trembling along his nerves. He stepped forward and knocked loudly on the hotel door. For a time there was no response, and he reached to use the heavy knocker again, then paused as a light was flicked on showing a faint crack of yellow illumination under the door. A moment later, shuffling steps sounded from somewhere beyond. They came nearer. A chain rattled eerily and a key clicked in the lock. The door opened.

O'Connell blinked as the light fell full on him. For an instant he could make out nothing beyond the fact that there was somebody squat standing in the open doorway, regarding him curiously. Then the other moved forward and peered closely at him.

'Yes?' muttered a thick voice. 'What do ye want?'

'Sorry to bother you at this time of

night,' said O'Connell, feeling strangely uneasy. 'But I've just arrived from Cork and I'm looking for a place to stay.'

The hotel owner stared at him groggily for a few moments, blinking and massaging his eyes. 'From Cork, ye say? Well, come in. Ye gave me quite a start for a moment. It isn't very often I get visitors durin' the winter. I wasn't expectin' anybody, certainly not this time o' night.' He stood aside and waited for O'Connell to enter before closing the door. 'Ye'd better come into the dinin' room. I imagine yer hungry. An' I imagine a nip o' the hard stuff wouldn't go amiss. Go on, help yersel' to a drink from the cabinet while I make ye up a little somethin' to eat.'

O'Connell began to feel better, now that he was away from the brooding darkness that lay outside. He moved across the room and poured himself a neat vodka. He sipped the drink slowly and felt his body relax as the liquor spread out through his limbs to mingle with the heat from the fire.

A minute later the hotel owner

returned, carrying a tray piled with food which he placed carefully on the polished top of a table. 'There we are. I hope ye'll find that to yer satisfaction.'

'Thanks.' O'Connell began helping himself to the pork pies and sandwiches.

'I take it yer down here on business?'

O'Connell nodded and waited until he had finished his mouthful before answering: 'That's right. My name's O'Connell — Martin O'Connell. I received notification a few days ago concerning the — ' He stopped as he caught a glimpse of the expression on the other's face. The man was almost scared to death! What the hell was going on around here? First the solicitors, now the hotel owner.

'Jesus Christ almighty! So it's true! Yer old Paddy O'Connell's nephew! I've heard tell how he had one somewhere, but as we didn't see ye at the funeral I put it down to hearsay. An' I suppose ye'll be wantin' to take over the place now that it's yers.'

O'Connell shook his head. 'Not particularly,' he muttered. 'I've never seen it, except for a glimpse on the way here, but it doesn't look to be the kind of place I'd want to take up residence in. Far too remote for me.'

'Thank God for that,' said the other fervently, with a rather loud and somewhat forced laugh. He sat down.

'It would seem from what I've be able to gather that the place has earned an evil reputation for itself around here,' said O'Connell.

'That it has. Now I won't go as far as to claim that it killed yer uncle. I'm well aware o' the fact that the medical authorities are satisfied that heart failure was the cause o' death. An', o' course, he was an old man. A very old man. But there are several ways in which a man can die so that it has all the appearances o' heart failure. Fright, for instance. But then — I hope ye don't mind me sayin' this — he was a strange man. Very strange. Now please don't think that I'm bein' impertinent, but no one knows what exactly went on in that house. No man, anyway. Except, perhaps your uncle. An' o' course he's dead now.'

'So I take it you believe in all these

tales about witchcraft and demons?'

'And what if I do? There are things that happen out here which would make yer blood freeze. Ye should know that Ireland isn't all leprechauns an' tales o' lucky widow's sons. There's an ancient evil in the land that's been here since time immemorial.'

O'Connell thought for a moment. He liked to believe that he was a rational, pragmatic kind of man. However, it could be that in places such as this people still adhered to and believed in the old ways — the pagan fears with which primitive man had regarded the gods of evil. Perhaps they thought the wickedness was still there, waiting to be released.

'Aside from what yer uncle got up to in that old house, there's another story concernin' it. An ancient legend, I suppose ye'd call it, though there's evidence aplenty to support the truth o' the details.'

'Go on.' O'Connell was interested. No doubt this was what Hayes had alluded to.

'Sometime durin' the seventeenth century, yer uncle's house was the residence o' the De Marcey family. About that time, witchcraft, as we call it today, was a common thing in these parts. Even the doctors themselves used certain ritualistic practices which might seem like sorcery to us today. The name o' the particular witch who inhabited this area is not recorded, but it's quite clear that she was taken before Sir Riordan De Marcey for trial, an' ordered to be hanged for her foul practices. The execution took place on the cliffs in front o' the mansion, overlookin' the sea. Before she died, the hag uttered a curse on the family an' swore that any heir would be born an abomination. A little over a year later, a son was born an', as the witch had said, he was a monster; a freak. Naturally, none o' this was supposed to leak out into the village, but there were countless stories o' strange happenings. Ghastly screams an' terrible cries in the dead o' night. God alone knows why the creature was allowed to live. Apparently he was kept locked in a room in the north wing. Altogether, he lived for twenty-three years.'

'I can understand the reason the house had such an evil reputation, but surely all of this happened over three hundred years ago,' said O'Connell. He didn't for one minute believe in curses, but it was quite possible that such a story had evolved from something related. It was fairly understandable that a deformed child would be hidden, kept out of sight for fear of shaming the aristocratic family. The possibility that his uncle's mansion had housed, or rather imprisoned, such an unfortunate made him uneasy.

'Well, there's a little more to the tale. Ye see, one night three o' the folk from Bantry decided to attempt to get into the place. Why exactly they went, I can't say. Curiosity, I suppose. Several hours passed before they returned to the village. Two of them were half-dead with fright an' the other was completely insane. The villagers could learn nothin' from them. Nothin' at all. There were all dumb. The fright had robbed them o' the power o' speech. After that, no further attempts were made to enter the house. It was shunned, left strictly alone.'

O'Connell finished his vodka. 'So what became of — ?'

'The abomination? Well, somehow he got out. How exactly, no one knows. But his body was washed up with the tide a couple of days later. A terrible, ghastly thing to be sure. They buried him a little further along the peninsula in a small unmarked grave overlookin' the sea. An' with his death, the title o' the De Marceys died too. No other son was born, and the house passed into other hands.'

'It's certainly a gruesome little tale,' commented O'Connell. 'But as I said earlier, all of this happened, if indeed it happened at all, hundreds of years ago.'

'Several people have had the house since then, but no one has stayed there very long. Apart from your uncle, that is. Some complained o' the oppressive atmosphere o' the place. Others were a little more specific.'

O'Connell glanced up sharply. 'What do you mean by that? Do you mean that they saw something?'

'Well . . . not exactly. Apparently they *heard* things. Several claim that they were wakened durin' the night by odd noises. Heavy, shufflin' footsteps in the corridors. Strange screams an' groans that started as soon as night came an' were sometimes heard even durin' the day. Odd marks were discovered on the floors and walls. Windows an' doors opened o' their own accord. An' from what I was told, the vast majority of these people had never heard o' the legend, so it can't be put down to imagination.'

O'Connell yawned. 'I'll take a look around the place tomorrow afternoon.'

'As ye will. But now I think ye'd better get yersel' to bed. If ye'd follow me, I'll take ye to yer room.'

* * *

Golden winter sunlight poured through the windows as O'Connell made his way downstairs towards the kitchen in the hope of getting some breakfast.

The hotel owner was there along with his wife, a small wrinkled woman with greying hair and thick glasses. She removed a crumpled cigarette from her mouth before speaking.

'Good mornin' to ye. So yer the young man from London who has come to take over the mansion? Well, ye look as though ye've got more sense than what yer uncle had, anyway. He was a fool to stay in that place. I always said so, an' I always will. No doubt my husband told ye o' what happened up there.' Deftly, she returned her cigarette to her mouth and sloppily cracked two eggs into a frying pan.

O'Connell nodded. 'It doesn't scare me, if that's what you mean.'

'I can see ye don't believe much o' it.'

'Please, take a seat,' said the hotel owner, gesturing to a chair. The table was already set out.

O'Connell sat down, noticing with revulsion the rather slapdash way in which the woman was cooking his breakfast. The ash from her drooping cigarette looked ready to fall into the frying pan at any moment. 'My personal opinion is — ' He stopped, then began again with a different tone. 'You people have lived here all your lives, and your ancestors before you, possibly as far back as you can conceivably remember. These legends have been instilled into your mind, gaining power and strength with every succeeding generation. Now you can no longer differentiate between that which is fact and that which is legend.'

'I just hope, for yer sake, that ye don't end up payin' for yer ignorance,' said the woman, messily buttering some toast. 'An', as it happens, we moved here from Dublin twenty years ago.'

There was little O'Connell felt he could say by way of response. Instead, he sat in silence and waited for his breakfast. Once it was ready, he began to eat ravenously. The food was tasty despite the dubious method of its preparation, but at the back of his mind there was the odd little feeling that something horrible had happened, or was going to happen, to him. He tried desperately to think what it could be, but for a long while it eluded him. Then he remembered.

During the night he had had a nightmare about a dark, dead, long-haired body swinging monotonously to and fro at the end of a rope, suspended from a towering gibbet that was there one minute and gone the next. Something that had appeared in the moonlight as a figment of his overwrought imagination. Or was it a warning — an omen, maybe? He thrust the dark thought into the far recesses of his mind and concentrated on his food.

★   ★   ★

It had just gone eleven o'clock when he walked into the small offices of the firm of solicitors in Killarney and was shown into the presence of Henry Ryan, a tall, thin man with greying hair and a self-possessed bearing that impressed itself most strongly on O'Connell. Here, he thought inwardly, was a man who would have no time for the superstitious claptrap he had been fed thus far. A man with a positive outlook who would give him straight answers to his questions.

'Now, Mr O'Connell. I've been expecting you to call. I was informed of your intent to come out here to view the property by your solicitors in London.

No doubt you'll be wanting some information regarding this place which your uncle, the late Patrick O'Connell, bequeathed you in his will.'

'That's correct.' O'Connell eased himself comfortably into his chair. Somehow the staid surroundings of the office gave him an inward feeling of sanity. 'I've heard several strange stories regarding what's supposed to have happened there since I arrived last night.'

'I can well imagine that. Unfortunately, you'll find that many of the people in Bantry and the surrounding area hold to their fixed beliefs far more tenaciously than you or I. That said, I wouldn't blame them too much, Mr O'Connell, at least not until you've been up to the house. Look around for yourself. See it as your uncle must have seen it, forty years ago when he first moved in, and ask yourself this: Is this place peopled with devils? I'd be interested to know what you think, for I must confess to having an interest in such things.'

'Regarding this legend about the De Marceys' deformed son . . . '

'That's no legend. He did exist. There's not the slightest shadow of doubt about that.'

O'Connell gulped nervously. To have at least part of the story verified in such a manner just compounded his dark thoughts. 'But there must be something more to it that keeps these people away from the place.'

'Maybe there is something. This story — this legend, if you like — has been at the back of these people's minds for countless years now. A story told at night, handed down from father to son, from mother to daughter. You know how it goes. And it's my belief that your uncle's death brought matters to a head. There are still some doubts in the minds of these people regarding the nature of his death.'

'I was told it was heart failure,' said O'Connell, managing to keep his voice steady. 'Are you trying to tell me it was something different?'

'No, not at all. Please don't get me wrong. As far as I'm concerned, it was heart failure. However, I . . . I saw him myself when they brought his body down to the village, and . . . '

O'Connell felt suddenly cold and uncomfortable. He glanced wonderingly at the other. 'Go on,' he prompted. 'Is there something I should know about?'

'There's nothing really,' muttered the other defensively. 'Perhaps I shouldn't have said anything. But when I saw your uncle — and please bear in mind that I'm not medically trained — if I had been asked the cause of death, I doubt whether I would have put it down to heart failure. There was an expression on his face that . . . that I never want to see again on any man, living or dead.'

'Then there is something up there.'

Ryan shrugged his shoulders. 'I can't say for certain.'

'Well damn it all!' O'Connell thumped his fist down hard on the desk. 'I'm going to go up there and find out for myself.'

'Are you sure that would be wise?'

'You bet.'

'Mr O'Connell, I wonder if you fully realise what it will cost you to go up there alone and stay in that house until something happens.'

'I don't understand. One minute you say you don't believe in any of this, the next you're saying that by going there I may be putting my life in danger. Which is it?' O'Connell looked angrily at the solicitor.

'I'm just telling you what I thought when I saw your uncle dead like that. Maybe it *was* just a heart attack, I don't know.' Ryan sighed. 'I can see that you're determined to go up there, and I'm prepared to take you part of the way.' He reached into a drawer and removed a bunch of keys, then handed them over. 'You'll need these.'

O'Connell stood up and reached for them. Feeling suddenly glad that he had made a decision, he headed for the door.

'I'll meet you at the turnoff in Bantry at say, five o'clock.'

With a curt nod, O'Connell turned and headed out of the office, walking quickly to the sunlit side of the street, where he made his way past the tiny shops and

cafés. Despite the bright morning sunlight, the wind was cold on his face as he
headed back to his parked car.

⋆ ⋆ ⋆

It was dark by five o'clock and bitterly
cold. O'Connell was standing at the
turnoff with a heavy torch in his hand and
an overnight bag resting at his feet, trying
to suppress the unsettling thoughts that
were roiling within his mind. He saw
approaching headlights and guessed that
it was Ryan. A moment later a car pulled
up beside him. The passenger door was
opened and the lawyer looked out at him.
    'Everything ready, Mr O'Connell?'
    O'Connell climbed inside, his bag on
his knees. 'Lead the way.'
    The drive up to the house took only ten
minutes, but in the darkness O'Connell
felt increasingly uneasy. On their right-
hand side the coastal edges of the low
cliffs took form, sloping down to the
frothing waves below. In places the road
began to dip and writhe, jutting outwards
until it seemed as though it stood poised

97

over the booming sea itself.

'As you can tell, this road isn't often used, certainly not since a bad storm a couple of years ago,' Ryan explained. 'A whole section a little further on broke away and swept a couple of cars into the sea. It's too dangerous for regular traffic now. Only the lighthouse-keeper out at Sheep's Head Point has reason to come out this way.'

The wind had picked up in strength; and out here, on this exposed finger of headland, it battered against the car. Flashes of lightning swept the distant horizon. Droplets of rain began to spatter the windscreen.

'And here we are.' Ryan brought the car to a stop.

O'Connell bent his head and looked out of the window. A wave of nausea threatened to grip him, pulling his muscles taut and rigid. Then he forced himself to look up. There in front of them, beyond a large wrought-iron gate, lay the forbidding spectre of his uncle's house. The sight of it brought an involuntary nervous gulp to his throat.

'Now that you've seen the place, are you sure I can't take you back to town?' said Ryan.

'That won't be necessary.'

'Very well. If you're set on staying, I won't try to persuade you not to, but take my advice. Keep away from the north wing — and if anything does happen, get out of that place and make your way back to Bantry. It'll be tricky making your way down the road in the darkness, but anything would be better than staying in that house if something does happen.'

O'Connell pulled up the collar of his raincoat. 'Thanks for the advice. But don't worry, I'll be down there in the morning, having my breakfast at the Bay Hotel. I'll give you a call just to tell you that all the phantoms are nothing but figments of your overwrought imagination.'

'I'm glad you're so sure,' said Ryan.

'Speak to you tomorrow.' O'Connell took his bag, opened the door and got out. Flicking on his torch, he watched as the lawyer carefully did a three-point turn and drove off, the red tail-lights visible in the darkness, glowing like a pair of evil eyes before disappearing. Then he turned and made his way slowly towards the gate.

Deep down, a part of him rather hoped that it would be locked and that he would be unable to open it. However, as he neared, he could see that it was slightly ajar. Shadows grew thick and huge along the short stretch of driveway that led up to the house, and he could discern the outlines of what appeared to be stunted willows on either side through which the wind gusted eerily.

It was all he could do to force his mind to work. Some hidden instinct warned him that something horrible was waiting for him, lurking in the shadows — something he must not see, because if he did it would drive him incurably insane. And in the morning, Ryan would come and find his stiff, dead body and take it down to the village as had happened with his uncle.

With a conscious effort, O'Connell pulled himself together and turned the front door key in the lock.

* * *

During the next half hour he carried out a quick but thorough investigation of the ground floor, intentionally beginning in the north wing which he had been told to avoid. As he had feared, there was no electricity, but he managed to find a couple of oil lamps hanging from the ceiling in one of the rooms which still functioned satisfactorily. These he lit and took with him to the huge dining room, placing them carefully on the large table that ran down the length of the room. He had brought tinned provisions with him, and after a brief meal he sat back and smoked a cigarette, almost defying anything unearthly to appear. Nothing did.

Smiling over this small triumph, O'Connell was just about to leave the room in order to start looking around the upper floors when he heard what sounded like a low chuckle of diabolical laughter. It seemed to come from just beyond the dining room door, out in the hall.

He tensed, trying to tell himself that it

had been nothing but the wind sighing through the windows. 'Is anybody there?' he cried into the dark opening. For a dreadful moment he thought he heard a creak as of someone going up the stairs.

Slipping the flashlight into his pocket, he picked up one of the oil lamps and made his way towards the great stairway. Climbing the stairs, he came out onto a broad landing, where he made his way along a veritable maze of corridors towards the opposite side of the building, to the side overlooking the wild cliffs and the lashing sea. The oil lamp threw huge grotesque shadows on the walls and ceiling. It seemed to O'Connell that something else — a great blob of darkness — followed him close behind, never coming out further than the corner of his vision, so that he was never able to see it properly. Several times he jerked his head round to stare at it, but always as he did so it vanished, drifting and fading away into a mere blur of normal shadow. He felt the fear and tension begin to surge up within him again.

For the next ten minutes, he wandered

around the upper floor. Finally, deciding that he would rest in one of the bedrooms, he locked the door, checked the window was tightly shut, took off his coat, draped it over the back of a heavy chair, and lay down on the huge bed. For the moment, at any rate, he believed himself safe.

The wind continued to howl outside, and the rain pattered strongly at the window, but inside all was still and quiet. Cold yellow moonlight played in strange distorted patterns across the rails at the end of the bed. O'Connell watched it idly for several moments, then rolled over on his side. His heart was still racing a little within his chest, but with an effort he ignored it. He closed his eyes and felt himself drifting off.

He slept for two hours. What brought him awake at the end of that short time, he didn't know. He had been in the middle of a wild dream, a nightmare, in which he was running down dank corridors, slipping and sliding in a vain attempt to escape from a misshapen black shadow that lumbered and shouted and had life when there should have been none.

Suddenly he found himself sitting bolt upright on the edge of the huge bed, his muscles and nerves stretched to the utmost. He felt weak and shaky. His whole mind bubbled and hummed with that peculiar mixture of shock and palpitation which comes after a close shave with disaster.

At first there was nothing to explain the sudden, unexpected awakening. The yellow patch of cold moonlight was still there, flooding into the centre of the room. It had moved a little across the uncarpeted floor, but that was all. It blanked out for an instant as a racing cloud sped across the sky, then it came back. The wind whistled a little dirge to itself as it blew around the window frame.

Then the window began to rattle furiously, banging and clattering as though something was trying to get in. One of the small panes of glass shattered. O'Connell leapt to his feet in alarm.

Suddenly the door handle rattled. A dull, throaty groan and an evil croaking noise came from beyond.

Panic threatened to overwhelm him. He was shaking inside and outside, a scream developing deep within his lungs.

The handle was tried again. There came a low, bubbling murmur which built itself up to a grating shriek, finally dying again into a sighing whimper, barely distinguishable from the wind.

Then whatever it was that was outside began to move away. O'Connell could hear its clumsy dragging movement over the smooth stone floor of the corridor outside. It was as though a heavy wet sack was being hauled along the passage. Madness threatened to consume him as in his mind's eye he visualised a loathsome thing lumbering along the maze of passages, trailing a length of shackled chain, a huge double-bladed axe in its hand. A murderous malformed creature, doomed and undying, born to be a monstrosity due to a witch's curse.

But even as he thought that it had gone, it began to come back.

He was caught in this room, being hunted by something he couldn't see, something he dared not see. No doubt the very same thing that had driven his uncle to madness, then killed him!

The door handle shook ever so slightly, as though the thing outside knew that someone was in the room and was trying the door experimentally. Then a croak of savage anger shattered the silence. Something heavy crashed against the woodwork. The door trembled. Another crash and the framework began to splinter.

With a scream, O'Connell backed towards the window.

And then the door fell in as something cowled and loathsome appeared in the doorway. A short, hunchbacked shape, one arm long and covered in filthy bandages, the other crooked and stunted. Under the hood, the contours revealed that the fiend's head was disproportionately large and bulbous. A slavering, grinning mouth stretched widely from ear to ear like that of a frog. Unsightly boils and weeping sores covered what patches of skin were visible.

Mumbling loudly, the mutant progeny of Riordan De Marcey reached out towards O'Connell. The stench of leprous decay struck his nostrils as he lost consciousness.

⋆ ⋆ ⋆

When he came to, O'Connell found himself propped in a large chair in a dank, vaulted chamber which he immediately assumed was beneath the house. Light came from an oil lamp which rested on a table strewn with papers and old-fashioned scrolls, books and other strange pieces of paraphernalia. On the walls he could see faded manuscripts and diagrams of a weird and esoteric nature. Nearby was a large bookcase filled with dusty and cracked books, the titles of which he couldn't make out from where he was.

Fear leapt into his mind as he recalled the horror that had barged into his room, forcibly propelling him from the chair. He had to get out of here. He moved towards the only door, and was just about to open it when he heard once again that nightmare shuffling sound as the deformed creature approached.

Knowing that there was nothing else for it, he searched around in vain for some kind of weapon. Suddenly the door creaked open and the diseased, misshapen monster stood framed in the doorway.

'What do you want from me?' O'Connell screamed, fighting back his revulsion.

The slavering freak gave a pitiful moan and pointed to the table with a fleshy hand.

O'Connell looked to where it indicated, his eyes drawn to a sheet of paper. He edged towards it, his eyes widening as he saw that it was a letter — addressed to him! He picked it up and began to read the spidery, barely legible words:

To my nephew Martin,

For many years I have dwelt alone in this house, living a life of seclusion whilst outside the people persist in their belief that I am a warlock engaged in occult practices. And whilst they are correct to some degree, I have never harmed another fellow being. Indeed, I have spent the better part of my life here researching a way in which I can free the poor tormented soul of Malachi De Marcey, the so-called monster that haunts this house. It is my belief that he can only obtain peace if the true evil which plagues this house — the witch, Magreg Doherty — is destroyed. Contained within the passages of the Book of Shadows you will find the necessary rite which, if performed correctly, should banish her once and for all. My health is poor, and if I should die before I have completed my task, I ask you to take on this burden for the sake of an innocent soul.

Your uncle,
Patrick

For a moment, O'Connell didn't know what to think. This account from his uncle turned everything on its head. He shuddered as he looked up and stared at the hideous abomination that waited expectantly nearby, realising that his uncle had devoted his studies to seeking a way of freeing it. Had it been pity on his uncle's part? Now that he had the strength of nerve to gaze at the other's ugliness, he did feel the faint stirrings of sympathy for its plight. Through no fault of its own it had been cursed to live, and die, and live again in a dreadful manner. It had been blameless, maliciously hexed from the moment of its creation due to the actions of its father.

And now it had fallen to O'Connell to seek a means of ending its three-hundred-year-old torment. Either that, or he could just leave. For something told him that now that Malachi had brought him down here and revealed to him the mystery surrounding this house, the creature wouldn't harm him or prevent him from leaving. He was simply watching him, a look of supplication in his eyes.

★　★　★

Shivering against the chill wind, O'Connell turned up his coat collar upon seeing the approaching lawyer's car. It was morning, and the winter sky was dark and menacing, thunderous almost. A direct contrast to how it had been this time yesterday. The car pulled up at the entrance of the Bay Hotel and Ryan got out. O'Connell could tell that the other was relieved to see him. No doubt he had been worried that he wouldn't have made it alive through the night.

'Mr O'Connell. I must say how pleased I was to get your phone call. I'll freely admit that after I left you last night, I thought it would take the services of a good medium to hear from you again.'

'Sorry to disappoint you.' O'Connell gave a wry grin and stepped forward. 'I take it you brought the spades?'

'Yes, but can you tell me what this is all about?'

'I can, but to be honest with you I don't know whether you're going to believe a word of it.' Upon seeing the somewhat shifty look they were being given by a couple of elderly villagers across the street, O'Connell gestured to the car. 'Maybe it would be best if we talk inside.'

'Fine.' The lawyer got back into his car and waited for O'Connell to join him.

'Last night, I encountered the ghost of Malachi De Marcey — the spirit of the deformed offspring of Riordan De Marcey. He took me down to a secret study in which my uncle kept many of his books on demonology and black magic.'

'You're joking, right?

'No. I'm deadly serious.' Through the windscreen, O'Connell could see that the two elderly villagers were still watching them. It was obvious that news had got round the close-knit inhabitants of Bantry that old Paddy O'Connell's nephew was in town and that he had spent the night at his uncle's accursed house. 'I understand it's an unusual request, but I want you to accompany me to a site not that far from the house, close to Mount Seefin. From what Malachi told me, that's where his physical remains lie buried.' There was an edge of grimness to O'Connell's words.

'Surely you don't mean to dig them up?' Ryan looked worried.

'That's exactly what I plan on doing.'

'But why?'

'Once the remains have been exhumed, I'm supposed to recite some spell or other from an old grimoire called the *Book of Shadows*. According to my uncle, that's the only way of ending Malachi's torment. Think of it as an exorcism of sorts.'

'You're serious about this, aren't you?'

O'Connell nodded. 'Look at it this way — only if I can rid the house of this spectre will I ever manage to sell it. But it's not just the money. My uncle devoted much of his life to trying to help this poor being. I feel duty-bound to see this task through. Sure, I could just drive to Cork and get the next flight back to London; try and forget about everything out here. But I'd be forever thinking about that doomed soul, haunted by the guilt that I walked away when I should have helped.'

Ryan regarded him worriedly. 'It sounds . . . crazy.'

'I understand if you don't want to be any part of it. It doesn't really concern you.'

Ryan sighed. 'I was one of the few people who stayed in touch with your uncle. He was definitely a bit strange, but he was a good man. If he thought this wretched ghost was worth saving, then I suppose I can do my bit to help. I'd not sleep at nights anyway after this if I just refused.'

'Right.' O'Connell gave the lawyer a thankful slap on the shoulder. 'The sooner we start this, the sooner we'll get it done. Let's get up to the house.'

★ ★ ★

O'Connell had left his companion waiting at the outside gate, for now that he had confirmed that the place was genuinely haunted, the other had steadfastly refused to enter. After a few minutes he returned, the weighty tome under one arm.

Ryan opened the car boot and took out two spades, then walked over. 'Is it my imagination, or is it getting darker?' He cast a worried glance to the heavens. It was still only mid-morning, but an unnatural darkness had crept across the sky, bringing an eerie presence to the desolate, windswept headland. A fierce wind had picked up, whipping the waves below them into a frenzy, sending them crashing against the black seaweed-draped rocks.

'It is getting darker.' Taking one of the spades, O'Connell started to go around the back of the house.

Reluctantly, Ryan followed, keeping his eyes down, fearing to look up at the numerous windows. Some were shuttered and many were broken, and it was at these that he imagined something grotesque and unearthly stood staring down at them, watching their movements with malign purpose.

The grounds at the rear of the house were overgrown and neglected. Cracked, weed-covered paving stones soon gave way to a long stretch of muddy lawn. To one side lay an abandoned summerhouse now in an advanced state of decrepitude, its skeletal framework festooned with crumbling vines. It was in there, many years ago, that Ryan had first met Patrick O'Connell, and for some terrible reason he had a sudden image of the old recluse's face peering out from inside, his look the same as that he had seen on his corpse the day it had been brought from the house.

'Be careful. It gets quite uneven here,' warned O'Connell. 'Apparently my uncle didn't think much of gardening.'

'I take it that book's written in English?' asked Ryan as they approached a rusty metal gate set into the high garden wall.

'Latin.'

'Can you read it?'

O'Connell turned. 'Means nothing to me, but I should be able to pronounce the words. I think that's all I need to do.' Having now reached the gate, he pushed it open.

Before them, a mile or so distant, loomed the dark hump of Mount Seefin. They headed towards the black mound, their surroundings becoming grim and threatening. An almost tangible sense of dread befell them with every step; and no matter how hard O'Connell tried to tell himself that he was doing the right thing, it seemed as though he was waging a losing battle. Deep down an intense sense of foreboding began to pull at his common sense, urging him to get away from this godforsaken place whilst there was still time to do so.

After ten minutes they had covered half a mile, reaching the base of the low mountain where a lone lightning-scarred oak tree could be seen, its branches grotesquely twisted.

'What exactly are we looking for?' asked Ryan. It had started to rain, and he was having serious misgivings about being there. The wind was intensifying, and at times he was sure he heard a distant wailing that set his teeth on edge.

'That!' O'Connell replied, pointing to the tree. Eagerly he jogged over to it. To one side, protruding from the ground like the tooth of some buried prehistoric monster, was a pointed rock. Now that he was close he could see others forming a small circular arc. In all, the stone circle was little more than six feet in diameter, the taller stones no higher than his shoulders. They had obviously been placed here rather than having been deposited by the action of nature. 'This must be the place.'

They began to dig in the very centre of the circle, and it was not long before Ryan's spade hit something with a dull thud. A little more excavation revealed a large wooden casket in an almost crumbling state. It was firmly embedded in the claggy soil, and they decided to try to open it in situ rather than digging the whole thing out. O'Connell took aim and carefully drove the edge of his spade into one corner. It splintered fairly easily, and they used the spades to break away almost all of the lid.

In the poor light they could see a collection of discoloured bones and the ragged, all but disintegrated remains of some clothing. For a moment O'Connell stood staring into the shattered funerary container, his eyes unreadable. 'Such a long time to wait for release,' he muttered quietly.

'Do you read the incantation or whatever it is now?' Ryan asked nervously. The cold wind and dark, almost twilight, sky was getting to him. He wanted nothing more than to return to the welcoming lights of Killarney and the reassuring peace of his office. This was a grim business and no mistake.

'Yes, the words should work.'

Now that that bones had been exhumed, the two men clambered out of the shallow grave they had uncovered.

O'Connell picked up the book and turned to the marked page. He began a widdershins perambulation around the stone circle. Speaking loudly to raise his voice over the now howling wind, he began to recite the Latin words.

Ryan watched with mounting apprehension. The wind was catching at his clothing like a spectral hand tugging at him. Twice he had whipped round, expecting to see some ghastly apparition, and he was now certain that there was a voice screeching in the wind. He had no wish to see the ghost of Malachi De Marcey and was praying that it would not appear. He kept his eyes on O'Connell and away from the bones. After a few moments, he realised that although the other held the open book in his hands, he was not looking at the page — and yet the incantation continued to roll out of his mouth.

O'Connell's eyes had become fixed and he seemed oblivious to the gusting wind. His voice was changing too, the Anglicised accent becoming more strongly Irish, and with a different, menacing tone. A moment later the book slipped unheeded from O'Connell's hands, and yet he continued to speak the incantation.

Ryan took an involuntary step backwards and stumbled on the uneven ground. He glanced down automatically and saw the bones begin to stir. They were moving, jerkily at first, but then they snapped together to form a skeleton. As O'Connell uttered the final words, Ryan could not stop himself from crying out: 'This is wrong! That can't be De Marcey; you said he was small and deformed.'

'Malachi De Marcey was indeed a horror to behold,' O'Connell replied, lifting his spade once more. 'His half-sister Magreg, however, was a normal, God-fearing woman until Riordan De Marcey, angered by the mere existence of his illegitimate daughter, turned his fury on her and decided to hang her as a witch.'

'I . . . I don't understand!' Ryan stammered. The wind was shrieking round the stones so loudly that he could hardly think. The rain turned black and oily.

'These are her bones, her restless remains, and she will soon be returned to life!'

'But how will that free Malachi?' Ryan shouted, wiping the foul dampness from his face.

O'Connell's face was twisting and contorting. There was malice and madness in his eyes. 'It won't. That half-wit would never have had the will to survive death.' He raised the spade. 'I only need flesh now to complete my resurrection. I will have the life denied me by my murderous father.' The terrified solicitor ducked the blade that swung swiftly at him, then turned to run.

Suddenly the skeleton rose from the ground and grabbed hold of him. The last thing he saw was the wickedly grinning skull before the mud-encrusted bladed edge of the shovel sped towards his head.

★ ★ ★

With the sacrifice complete, O'Connell stood perfectly still, his eyes blank and unseeing. The wind screamed louder than ever, and an eldritch green mist seeped from the ground, shrouding the bones. The shallow grave was becoming boggy as that terrible foul rain continued to fall. The smoke cleared, and in its place there appeared a young, long-haired, naked woman. She drew in a deep, exultant breath and laughed.

O'Connell tumbled to the saturated ground, her possession of him no longer necessary. She looked at him without much interest. He had been of use, as had his uncle, although the latter had long resisted her attempts at possession using magic of his own. If she had not found a way to manipulate the old demonologist, she would still be a ghost. The apparition she had created of poor, witless Malachi had worked well, until the old man's health had finally given out. She had been fortunate that the nephew was as stupidly kind-hearted as his uncle and that he had easily fallen for the fake letter she had penned.

O'Connell groaned and began to shake as he came to and saw the bloody remains of Ryan and the triumphant figure of Magreg Doherty, risen from the dead, standing over him. Something snapped inside his head, and he was shrieking as he tried to scramble away from the terrible scene, clawing his way forward on the mud.

With a deathly wail, the banshee — for such she had become through the centuries of bitterness, denied a proper burial in sanctified ground — stopped his heart. Turning her back on the lonely grave in which she had been interred, she strode towards the De Marcey mansion, hers now by right of birth and by right of conquest; inky, night-black fluid streaming down her pale body.

The Darkest Witchcraft

The power of hexerei could kill livestock — but could it be used to commit murder?

A hard rain beat down against the windscreen of the battered old car as it made its way slowly along the winding forested mountain road, the engine protesting shrilly under the shaking bonnet. Behind the wheel, Harvey Peterson stared straight ahead, his eyes following the rugged contours of the surrounding countryside, striving to pick out any landmarks which could provide him with a clue as to how much further he had to go. This was only the second time he had been in these parts, well off the beaten track, and it was still possible that the old hatchet-faced hillbilly back at the last petrol station had intentionally given him wrong directions.

For almost three years now, he had been scouring the Appalachian Mountains of southern Pennsylvania and northern Virginia in an attempt to locate the origin of certain myths and legends.

All the way along the line, whenever he had questioned these suspicious, backward folk in their isolated hovels, trying to get information on their superstitions, particularly the working of their curses and witchcraft, most had shut up like clams and refused to answer his questions. Some had told him stories of what was supposed to have happened in the past, a hundred or so years earlier. But all the time, even as he had patiently listened and taken down notes, he had known that they were lying to him, making up the tales as they had gone on. Whether he would ever find anyone willing to tell him what he wanted to know was doubtful, but he was rapidly coming to the end of his patience.

Slowly he eased back the throttle of the car and sat back in his seat. It was a long, tortuous road. He had been driving now for close on four hours in the blinding rain, and his temper, which was not very good at the best of times, was beginning to get the better of him. If only the rain would stop, then he might be able to see exactly where he was; but with it battering incessantly against the windscreen like that, running down in a wash of water, which the solitary wiper couldn't hope to cope with, it was impossible to —

Instinctively his foot slammed down on the brake, bringing the car to a screeching stop. He had come to the top of a low rise. On one side of him the mountains rose huge and gaunt, towering above the car, the upper slopes dotted with firs held apart by huge grey boulders that looked as though they might come sliding down upon him at any moment, crashing down on to the narrow road, burying the car beneath an avalanche of rubble.

On the other side of the road, some five yards of so ahead of Peterson, a narrow, twisting track, barely wide enough for the car, wound away to the left. It was visible for a hundred yards or so before it vanished in mystery into the dense trees. He sat quite still in his seat, trying to think back to the time he had last been in this area a little over a year before.

He prided himself on his excellent memory, sharpened by several years of patient research into the old customs of these people. There had been a multitude of facts to be remembered, and so far his memory had never once failed him. But that track — it hadn't been there before, he felt reasonably sure of that. And even as he looked at it through the pouring rain, there seemed to be something different about it: the way it dipped and writhed in a series of sharp turns and twists, swaying on the low hillside and folding itself neatly away in the distance, bordered by dark trees almost as if it didn't want itself to be seen and was trying desperately to hide away from prying eyes. The sight of it sent a small shiver of apprehension through him. Somewhat ominously, there was no signpost — nothing to give any indication as to where it led.

Peterson ran a hand down his stubbled chin. There was something here that intrigued him more than he cared to admit. Thoughts formed hazily in his mind as his brain shuttled like a mad thing inside his head. One glance was sufficient for him to realise, quite conclusively, that this was no new road constructed during the year since he had last been out this way.

He tried desperately to remember. A tiny voice at the back of his mind whispered at him to ignore it, to drive on to where he had been going before he had seen the road. After all, he couldn't possibly expect himself to remember every road and track that led off this twisting pass climbing through the hills.

He was about to start the engine and drive off when his gaze was drawn back to the turning. Looking at the road again, he felt his mouth suddenly go dry. In his mind he saw the numerous suspicious mountain folk who had watched him from every crude shack and rusting trailer along the road, peering at him from behind curtained windows. Men, crotchety and usually drunk on moonshine; women who were often as bad as the men and children, uneducated and dressed in rags. There was something *unwholesome* about this entire area — something indefinable, but there nonetheless, under the surface.

Damn them, Peterson thought fiercely, gritting his teeth. They were all purposefully keeping this knowledge from him. Had they guessed at the truth behind his questioning? Maybe they were merely being reticent, not wanting to talk about these local superstitions for fear of ridicule from an outsider such as he. Whatever the cause, in all of his travelling he had found nothing to help him.

But there had to be someone who could and would give him the answers he was seeking. Vaguely, he had the impression that if he wanted these answers he would not find them along the main route. Civilisation and the modern age were rapidly making ingress here, even into the mountains among these hill people. Mining and logging companies were moving in, driving these folk out. Soon their territories would be nonexistent, and when they went, so too would their beliefs and customs, diluted and eventually forgotten in the morass of modern life.

He turned the car, listening to the comforting whirr of the engine under the bonnet, feeling the solid crunch of smooth stones under the tyres. The tension and the odd little feeling of bewilderment were growing within him. He stared straight ahead, following the rugged contours of the twisting surface.

Nothing seemed to move in front of him. No birds, no animals. It was as if the entire place was an uninhabited, dead land.

Lurching and bumping over the loose stones, he turned the car, tyres crunching on the loose gravel. Pressing the accelerator, he drove towards the mysterious track. The surface became even rougher as it grew narrower.

Breathing more easily, Peterson relaxed and allowed his mind to run over the events that had led to him being here, in this godforsaken wilderness miles from anywhere: a pitiless, hungry land that had bred a race of people who had come over from Europe to settle, bringing all of their old customs and legends with them.

It was these which interested him more than anything else. Since as far back as he could remember, he had wanted to know more about these old tales; to probe into them with the fine-toothed comb of science, rejecting those that were obviously false, mere fabrications, but fastening tenaciously onto anything that might hold a grain of truth.

Sometimes his handful of friends had warned him against going too deeply into such things, or else had laughed outright at his preoccupation, informing him that he was mad and that he was wasting his time. *Well, to hell with them!* He smiled grimly to himself as he rested his hands lightly on the wheel. Once he learned the truth behind the curses — the hexerei — perhaps he could perform them himself, for that was his ultimate aim. Then he would be in a position to show them all. Then it would be his turn to laugh.

A feeling of sudden, sadistic pleasure pulsed through him at the thought, and his foot pressed a little harder on the accelerator as though anxious to be getting on with the task of finding someone who could provide him with the knowledge he desired.

The rocky surface of the road became even rougher as he progressed. Even the surrounding terrain changed. The trees loomed thick around him, throwing grotesque eldritch shadows before him. Weirdly etched boulders hung over the sides of the road, cutting off all view of what lay beyond, even if he had been able to see clearly through the pouring rain. A distant peal of thunder rumbled along the horizon.

The car lurched again, seeming to spin sideways as Peterson fought for control. Madly he turned the wheel, gripping it with all his strength. Without even knowing it, he had reached a wooden bridge spanning a shadow-filled ravine.

For one terrible moment, it seemed as though the car hung poised on the edge of an abyss that dropped away for a hundred feet or more. Peterson had a glimpse of darkness where the rocks seemed to drop away into a deep nothingness, and the meandering course of a river far below him. Hell, why hadn't there been a sign of some kind to warn motorists of this?

He swore savagely as he pulled hard, trying to ease the car back, away from that terrible drop. Smoke rose as the front tyre spun without making purchase. Deep inside, there was the urge to scream, but no sound came out. Instead, it all seemed to bottle itself up in Peterson's throat, stifling him, so that he hung, gasping, onto the wheel.

Then the rear tyres caught, gripped, and held. The car lurched back onto the road again, twisted slightly as though some force had pushed against it, then righted itself.

Shuddering, Peterson pressed his foot down hard on the brake, bringing the vehicle to a halt. Only then did he relax and wipe the filming sweat from his face. His back was cold, and his fingers, he noticed, were trembling violently. Reaching into his pocket, he pulled out a cigarette and thrust it between his lips, lighting it with difficulty. Breathing the smoke down into his lungs, he got out of the car and appraised the bridge before him. It *looked* passable, providing he took it steadily.

He got back into his car. From his lowered driver's perspective, capable of seeing very little but the way ahead, he was now uncertain whether trying to get across was such a good idea. All it would take was for one of the supports to give way or for him to steer slightly off centre, and things could well prove disastrous. Was trying to find information about this superstitious belief really worth risking his life for?

Gently chewing his bottom lip, he pushed the gearstick forward and pressed down on the accelerator. The vehicle crept forward, rumbling over the thick wooden planking. The bridge was barely wide enough to take the car. Looking out of the near window, his heart skipped a beat as he realised just how precipitous this all was.

Agonisingly slowly, the car rolled forward. At one point something gave way and the back tyres lost their traction. Planks cracked and fell away. With a squeal of tortured wood and metal, a support buckled. Peterson envisaged the whole thing collapsing and the car plunging down, smashing onto the ravine floor and exploding in a crumpled fiery mass, with him trapped inside.

Then he was moving forward once more, clearing the bridge. After a moment he got out, took a deep breath, and pressed himself against the side of the car furthest away from the edge of the bridge. The rain spilled down in sheets, limiting his vision. The edge of the cliff wall seemed to be less than three feet away, and on the other side, as he well knew, it fell away without warning. It would be a sheer impossibility for him to turn the car here. And in the rain it would be suicide to attempt to travel for any distance in reverse. There was only one thing for it: to go on and see what lay ahead.

He shivered again, convulsively, studying the track in front of him. Rain lashed at him, plastering his hair to his scalp. A little further on, the track degenerated still further. He doubted whether he'd get the car down there.

Angrily, he opened the car door and switched off the engine. There was nothing else for it: he would have to go forward on foot. It was not a pleasant prospect, but one which was, unfortunately, unavoidable. Unless he dared turn around somehow and make his way back across the rickety bridge.

God alone knew how he was going to get back. Ahead of him stretched an eternity of stark ruin and rugged boulders that threatened to block his path even before he had started. Buttoning up his jacket, he strode purposefully forward, holding up his spirits with a physical as well as a mental effort. The chill wind clutched at his body with ripping, seeking fingers. The rain probed into his clothing until, within minutes, it was completely sodden, clinging uncomfortably around his body.

He stopped and tried to marshal his turbulent thoughts. How was it that he had seen no house, no farm of any kind all the way out here? Surely someone lived in these parts. Overhead, the racing storm clouds darkened ominously above the rearing rocks. And there was something chill and dead and empty about the way the wind sent them swooping low over the ground and spun little eddies of grey dust out of hidden corners, where the rain caught them and flattened them instantly to the wet ground. There was also something indefinably unnatural in the way the wind pulled at Peterson's coat and shivered along his body, as though striving desperately to possess him.

He began to walk rapidly, accelerating his stride a little. In the pit of his stomach there was a biting sense of alarm that he couldn't understand or define. There was no reason why it should be there, he told himself fiercely. Desperately, he tried to convince himself that there was nothing at all to be afraid of.

Then, rounding a bend in the snaking path, he came upon a ramshackle mountain cabin set well back on the slope of the hill. Apart from its advanced decrepitude, it didn't look any different from the scores of others he had visited during the past few months. In front of a long, low wooden shack, a front stoop had been built; and hanging from it on long strings were brilliant red peppers, sheltered from the rain by a wooden roof.

A thin column of smoke rose from the single chimney and lifted itself above the scrubbed pine, where it was immediately ripped away by the wind rushing down the side of the mountain and dissipated into blue threads. A few rain-bedraggled chickens were scratching about in the yard, and a scrawny, flea-bitten cur came growling towards him, grovelling on its belly in the muck.

Shivering, Peterson headed along the short path that the rain was rapidly turning into a quagmire. His feet slipped in the mud. Reaching the rickety wooden gate, he swung it open, then stopped short.

A tall, lean-faced, stubbled man stepped out of the shadows behind the house and walked forward a couple of paces, a double-barrelled shotgun held loosely in the crook of his arm, the barrels pointed straight at Peterson's chest. There was no mistaking the glint in the mountain man's eyes.

With an effort, Peterson forced a smile. It was several seconds before he could muster up the courage to speak. For all his dealings with these people, this was the first time anyone had greeted him with a gun. Marked suspicion and reticence, yes — but this . . .

'Ye lookin' fer somethin', mister?' There was marked animosity in the other's gruff voice. The held shotgun never wavered.

'In a way, yes,' called Peterson. 'I'm sorry to trouble you like this, but I seem to have lost my way. My car's stuck about a quarter of a mile back along the road and I'm afraid it'll take some time before I can move it. I was wondering if I might come in out of the rain and take shelter until this damned storm passes over.'

'Where are ye from?'

Peterson shrugged. 'Don't you think we might talk inside?' he suggested. 'There's no point in our standing out here, getting wetter every minute.'

The hillbilly seemed to pause, then lowered his shotgun just a shade and nodded. 'Very well. But only until the storm's passed o'er. That's all.' He grabbed the mongrel by the scruff of its neck and flung it to one side. With a yelp it slinked off.

'Fine. Thanks.'

The man led the way into the shack. Inside, there was a fire burning in the open hearth and a steel pot hanging on a ring over it. Placing his shotgun in the corner, he walked over to the plain wooden table.

'Are you all alone here?' asked Peterson. Some of the warmth from the fire was beginning to work its way into his body, loosening the taut muscles.

'That's right, an' I don't like any interference from outsiders. How ye managed to find this place, I don't know; but once the rain's off, ye git. And don't come back this way again.'

'There's no law that says where I must or mustn't go,' said Peterson defensively. He sat bolt upright in his chair. In his pocket he could feel the comforting weight of the revolver he always carried on such trips as these.

'We don't want yer kind around these parts,' said the old man harshly. 'This has been ma land since longer than I can remember, an' it's been in ma family since we settled here nearly three hundred years ago.'

Peterson looked interested. If only he could get the other to talk. 'That's intriguing,' he said very quietly, keeping his gaze fixed on the other's face. 'Then I suppose you've heard of some of the old legends that are common in this district.'

'Legends?' muttered the hillbilly. He glanced suspiciously at Peterson, and there was a curious expression on his features. 'What kind o' legends are ye talkin' about?'

'Oh, nothing in particular.' Peterson thought fast, trying to figure out the best way to handle this man. The first wrong thing he said and the other might take off for that shotgun in the corner. He didn't want to have to use the revolver in his pocket unless it was absolutely necessary. Inside his head, he could feel the little chills of apprehension that always crowded in whenever he was on the point of finding out anything. The more he thought about it, the more probable it seemed that this man sitting at the table in front of him knew something about the *hexerei*, if only he could get it out of him. But what if the old fool refused to talk?

Little bits of half-forgotten knowledge were filtering into Peterson's mind, forcing their way into his consciousness despite all his attempts to prevent it. Some of them made sense, some didn't. He was busy remembering all of the things he had heard concerning these old farmers of Dutch stock. There was only one family that had settled and tilled this piece of land for almost three hundred years that he knew of — the Horsts, who had come over here from Holland and settled in this area in 1668. Was it possible that this man was a descendant of that family?

He said quietly: 'I don't suppose your name would be Horst, would it?'

A strange light came into the old Dutchman's eyes. His face tightened. 'How do ye know ma name, stranger?' he growled.

'Just a guess. But you've told me all I want to know.'

The old man leaned forward over the table. He turned his head briefly as in the hearth a pine log cracked and popped, spitting a shower of flames up the wide chimney. 'Ye seem to know too much to be just a casual stranger in these parts. What is it ye want wi' me? An' how did ye find the road?'

'The road?' Peterson felt a faint tremor of fear deep down in his chest. So there *had* been something strange about that road. The thought drove all of the warmth momentarily out of his body. His heart almost stopped its heavy thudding behind his ribs, but with an effort he pulled himself together. 'You're right, of course,' he went on smoothly. 'I did come out here for a reason, although I'd no idea I'd be as fortunate as this. You see, over the past three years, I've been scouring this area trying to find someone who would tell me about the *hexerei*.'

'*Hexerei!*' For the first time, his saw fear in the other's face. 'Just what do ye know about that?'

'Quite a lot, I can assure you. But unfortunately, only legends. Nobody seems to be able to tell me anything about the facts. That's what I'm interested in, and I intend to get the answers. It's vitally important to me.'

'An' ye think anyone'll tell ye?' There was a sneering tone in the man's voice. He threw back his head and laughed loudly, the sound more of a dry cackle. 'Ye ought to know by now that nobody'll ever tell ye anythin' concernin' the *hexerei*.'

'But supposing I can persuade them?' said Peterson.

The other glanced up sharply at that. His face seemed to change abruptly. 'Just how do ye think ye can do that? I've only got to get that gun to put a stop to all o' yer schemes.'

'Somehow I don't think so.' Peterson barked out a harsh laugh. 'Now that I've found someone who really knows about the *hexerei*, nothing can stop me from learning it for myself.'

With a suddenness that almost took Peterson by surprise, the old man thrust back his chair and lurched for the shotgun in the corner. He had almost reached it when Peterson pulled out the revolver in his pocket and sent a shot mere inches past the hillbilly's head. The old man stopped abruptly and turned round slowly.

'There,' said Peterson quietly. 'I thought you'd begin to see things my way. I don't want to have to kill you, especially before I've learned everything I want to know, so I'd appreciate it if you'd put the shotgun away and just sit down. We can talk more freely if I don't have to hold this gun on you all the time.'

'Ye stupid, ignorant, stubborn fool!' The other spewed the words out. 'Do ye think I don't know what yer tryin' to do? Ye don't know the evil power yer playin' wi' once ye start probin' into the *hexerei*.'

'I think I do.' Peterson nodded his head. He still held the revolver pointed at the other's chest, as the old-timer lowered himself into the chair opposite him and sat with his body slumped despondently over the table.

'Ye've only heard the legends,' went on

the other. 'Ye've admitted that yersel'. What can ye know o' the horrors o' these curses?'

'I know that one of your ancestors, Abraham Horst, practised the *hexerei* over eighty years ago, if these legends are anything to go on, and that a woman who may have been your great-grandmother was burned as a witch because of it. Surely some of that knowledge must have been handed down to you. Ah, I can see from your face it has, so you needn't lie to me.'

'I wasn't goin' to lie to ye,' said the hillbilly sadly. He shook his head. 'It's just that ye've no idea o' the evil involved; the terrible things that can happen.'

'Then it's all true, after all.' Peterson eased his tight-fisted hold on the revolver. 'I want to know all about it. How it's practised, what results one might expect, everything.'

'Is that why ye've come here?'

'Of course. And bear in mind it's the *hexerei* — the black witchcraft — I'm interested in learning. Not any of that stupid pow-wowing stuff. I've spent my

149

time talking to the descendants of Mountain Mary over in the Blue Hills and they told me to come out here. So here I am. Besides, what other reason could there be for anyone to come to this godforsaken place?'

'Godforsaken is right,' said the old Dutchman quietly. 'And that's how it's been ever since ma family settled here. How could it be otherwise when this cursed kind o' witchcraft's been practised for three hundred years?'

'Exactly. And this is the only place in the world where I can hope to find out the truth. I'll make myself quite clear to you, for I intend my visit to be as brief as possible. I've no wish to remain here once I've learned everything I need to know.'

'Ye mean that ye intend to practise it yersel'?'

'Perhaps.' Peterson forced casualness into his tone. 'But perhaps we could talk better over a glass of something.' He nodded towards the array of high-necked bottles on the shelf at the end of the room, then got to his feet and took one down. 'That's better,' he said, pouring out two glasses of a thick molasses-like beverage. He pushed one towards the old Dutchman. 'Here, take one yourself. There's nothing like homemade liquor for loosening the tongue and jogging bad memories.'

The silence was suddenly oppressive. Outside, the rain was still beating against the windows and rattling against the roof overhead. Some fell in a sudden fury down the chimney and spat against the flames in the hearth.

'Look, mister, all I'm tryin' to do is warn ye against goin' on wi' this. As ye've already guessed, the *hexerei* is real. People can be cursed, if ye only know the right way o' goin' about it.'

'And you know the right way?' prompted Peterson harshly.

'I can't remember it all.'

'But there must be books. Your father must have had the knowledge handed down to him, and then passed it on to you.' Peterson's tone hardened. 'Don't try to stall with me. I'm not in the mood for it. I didn't come all the way out here or spend the best part of three years in this wilderness just for the fun of it. Too many people have been evasive whenever I've asked them questions. Oh, sure, they'd tell me that a couple of hundred years ago somebody was burned as a witch. They'd even go into sordid details as to what she'd done and how her victims had died because of her witchcraft. But nobody would tell me a single thing as to how to perform *hexerei*.'

'There are only a few who still know,' replied the old man. He gulped down his drink and sat back, regarding Peterson with malevolent eyes. Then his gaze flickered down to the gun in Peterson's hand, as though he were deliberating the chance of snatching it before he could use it.

'And you're one of them,' said Peterson harshly. 'But enough of this. Talk quickly! And the truth, mind — otherwise I'll be forced to use this. You understand?'

Horst nodded his head emphatically. There was a trace of fear in his deep-set eyes.

'If you can't remember all the details, there must be books on the subject.'

'There were.' Horst nodded again. 'But no longer. I burned 'em. They were evil things. It was better that they should be destroyed.'

'Burned them? You fool! Don't you realise how valuable they could have been?'

'To a man like yersel', you mean.' The old Dutchman smiled sadly. 'I realised that only too well, which was the reason why I burned 'em.'

'But you still remember how to do it?' There was a dread insistence in Peterson's voice.

'Aye, that I do.' Horst nodded reluctantly, licking his lips dryly. 'It's impossible to destroy the memory. Only death can do that.'

Peterson uttered a low sigh of relief and leaned back in his chair, picking up the glass of homemade liquor. He sipped slowly. There was a peculiarly pungent taste to it that he didn't recognise. He replaced the glass on the table. 'Very well. Are you going to show the hex to me, or do I have to force it out of you?'

There was a long, uneasy pause.

Hatred burned deep in Horst's eyes, as though a hidden devil had leapt up out of the dark depths and now stared out of him, naked and terrifying, just for an instant before vanishing again. 'I'm sorry that yer such a fool. Yer so blind that ye simply won't believe. That's what happened to the others. They didn't believe either.'

'The others?' Peterson felt a sudden qualm of uneasiness within him. Had there been others seeking this knowledge before him? He felt his mind spinning madly.

'Ye aren't the first to come after this terrible knowledge, ye know.'

Peterson was vaguely aware that all the time Horst's face was growing grimmer, more sober. There was a tired look on his features and a great bleakness about his eyes and lips.

'And what happened to them?'

'They died. That's why I want to warn ye against — '

Peterson stopped him with a negligent wave of the gun. 'Just perform the hex,' he said harshly. 'I'll take care of the rest.'

Horst shrugged his shoulders. Slowly he got up, walked over to the hearth, and placed several logs of pine wood onto the fire, kicking them down with his foot. The wood sparked a little, cracking as the flames caught.

'Very well. I can do no more. I've warned ye — that ought to be enough.'

Peterson pushed himself to his feet. Going over to the corner of the room, he picked up the old man's shotgun, removed the shells, and tossed the weapon out of the half-open window. 'Now,' he said hoarsely, 'we'll begin.'

The old Dutchman took a deep breath. Then he nodded. 'Come wi' me,' he said gruffly. All of the fight seemed to have drained out of him.

Peterson followed him outside. The rain had lessened appreciably, and the sun was beginning to break through the tattered strips of cloud that still clung to the horizon. The chill tenseness was back in his throat now, constricting it slightly. Very soon, he told himself fiercely, he would know the truth, if there *was* any truth in these ancient legends.

Hexerei! What a strange and oddly forbidding word it was. And what strange things it seemed to conjure up in his brain. He mulled the word over as he followed Horst over the rain-soaked yard at the back of the shack and into the small wood that crowded at the base of the gaunt mountain. He began to walk a little faster, trying to keep up with the other who strode ahead, never once looking back.

'I hope this isn't a trick,' Peterson said finally. 'If it is, it'll be the worse for you. Where are we going?'

Horst paused and turned his head. 'First we need the pine cross,' he said cryptically. 'Only then can we begin the hex.'

'Very well. But don't try to waste any time in the hope that some of your redneck friends will come. I saw nobody all the way here.'

A few moments later, Horst glanced about him as though making sure of his exact whereabouts, then took out a long-bladed knife. Going over to the nearest tree, he cut off a couple of short, straight branches, looked at them for a moment as if appraising their length and quality, then stuffed them into his shirt, replacing the knife in his pocket.

'Is that all?' asked Peterson, watching closely.

'Fer the moment.' The other nodded his grizzled head. 'Now we must go back and prepare the hex.'

There was a cloud of low mist hanging over the shack as they came back to it, Peterson picking his way carefully forward along the winding trail, the old man striding purposefully ahead, looking neither to the right nor the left, but staring grimly ahead.

'We'll need an animal,' said Horst.

'One of the chickens?'

'Aye, that'll do.'

After a few moments, Peterson managed to corner one of the scurrying chickens against the wooden fence. Bending swiftly, he scooped it up, holding it tightly against him, the pecking beak suddenly scratching across the back of his hand, drawing blood. Savagely, he handed it over. 'You ready to start now?'

'Aye, we might as well. I don't like this business at all, I tell ye. But the sooner it's o'er and done wi', the better I'll like it.'

'Then hurry. What comes next?' asked Peterson impatiently.

'First, these two twigs I took from the pine must be tied in the form o' a cross, like this.' Horst laid the two branches on the ground and tied them tightly together with a link of strong twine.

'Now what?'

'We must sprinkle the blood o' the creature to be hexed onto the cross.' Horst made a small cut in the chicken's leg, allowing the blood to drip onto the wooden cross. 'We must tie this chicken up now so that it can't escape. Then we must recite the chant o'er the cross.'

'And then? How will we know whether the hex has worked or not?'

'Ye'll see that fer yersel'.'

After tying the chicken to a small stake in the middle of the yard, they walked back into the shack. Peterson followed the other until they were back in the room with the fire spluttering in the wide hearth.

'Now we must begin,' said Horst thinly. 'The chant's easy enough to remember providin' ye've a good memory.'

'I have.' Peterson sat in the chair by the table and listened while Horst laid the wooden cross carefully on the floor and began to recite a peculiar monosyllabic chant, the pitch of his voice never varying. There was something about the rhyme that sent little shivers running up and down his back. For a long moment he sat quite still at the table, listening to the weird chant, watching the old codger swaying back and forth over the tiny wooden cross on the floor, his face twitching slightly, his eyes staring straight ahead, almost as though he were in some kind of trance.

Suddenly, the place seemed full of something that stung at the back of Peterson's nostrils, sending a little stab of terror into his brain. He jerked his head back with an almost physical violence, trying to remember the words the other was using. There was a sensation that something was happening behind his back that he ought to know about, something important. His brain persisted in stirring up a vast agglomeration of thoughts that didn't make much sense, but all the time it was storing away the words of the runic chant, memorising them for future reference.

Outside, the wind picked up in strength, howling around the house. The sky darkened as though something had passed over the face of the sun, blotting it out for a long moment. Peterson felt his brain reeling. But he had come this far to learn these things, and he intended to go through with it. Gritting his teeth, he leaned forward in his chair. With an effort, he found his voice. 'Is that all there is to it?'

Horst nodded. 'That's all,' he said slowly. 'Do you think ye've managed to memorise it?'

'Yes, I think so. But how do you know whether or not the hex has worked? Simply by going out and taking a look at the animal?'

'Not quite. We must hang up the cross an' wait. If the curse has been successful, we'll soon know.' Horst hung the wooden cross on a long piece of black thread and suspended it from one of the beams that ran across the ceiling. It dangled in front of them, moving slightly as the draught caught it. Almost as though it were alive, thought Peterson suddenly.

For a long moment, nothing happened. The cross swung gently back and forth like some grotesque pendulum, the tiny specks of blood from the chicken standing out slickly on the surface. Then, quite suddenly, there came the tiny curling of blue smoke. It was as if an invisible magnifying glass had been placed between it and the rays of the sun.

Peterson caught his breath. Then he felt a cold shudder run through his entire body.

'There,' said the old man. 'It's worked.'

Within seconds, the cross had flickered into flame. Slowly, the wood was consumed as a fire spread outwards, crackling a little.

'That's it,' said Horst with an odd little chuckle in his voice. 'I think ye'll find that the chicken's dead.'

Trembling a little, Peterson followed

161

the other out into the yard. The chicken they had tied to the small stake lay on its side, already stiffening. Going down on one knee, Peterson examined it carefully, finally satisfying himself that it was dead.

'Well? Are ye happy now?'

'Almost. There are just a few more questions I'd like to ask, and then I'll be on my way.'

'Very well. What are they?' Horst kept glancing over his shoulder as if afraid someone or some*thing* might come out of the shadowy trees and pounce upon him while he was not looking.

'Firstly, can anything be done for the victim to prevent the hex?'

Horst shook his head gravely. 'Once the cross has burned itself out, there's nothin' that can be done to save the victim.'

'I see.' Peterson nodded, satisfied. 'Just one other point. I can well believe that this hex will kill an animal. What about a person? Would that be equally successful?'

'A person?' There was a trace of incredulous fear in Horst's voice. 'So far as I know, this hex has never been used on a human bein'. To kill a neighbour's

162

animals, chickens an' goats, aye — but never a person.'

'Ah, then it might work?'

'I don't know.'

'Don't you think it might be a good idea to find out?'

Horst looked at him in shocked surprise. 'Just what is it ye want to do?'

'I thought I'd already made that clear. I want to see if this hex will work on a human being.'

'Yer mad! Crazy!' Horst leapt to his feet and stood looking down at Peterson, gripping the edge of the table, knuckles standing out whitely beneath the skin.

'Am I? Somehow I don't think so. Do you honestly believe I came here just to see this one demonstration of the hex? If so, you're a bigger fool than I took you for.'

'It won't work on a human bein',' shouted Horst frenziedly. 'I tell ye, it can't possibly have any effect.'

'Aren't you changing your mind a good deal?' said Peterson. He was smiling as he got to his feet.

'What do ye mean?' There was a trace

of fear in the old Dutchman's voice. 'What are ye tryin' to say?'

'Simply this. That second drink you had contained something that will very soon put you to sleep. Quite a tasteless and harmless drug, but sufficiently strong for my purpose. And once you're — '

'Why you — ' Horst hurled himself forward.

Before Peterson realised it, the other's fist had struck him full in the face, hurling him back against the table. It fell over with a crash and he found himself sprawling on the floor. Instinctively, he threw up his left arm to protect his face as Horst kicked viciously at him. The full weight of his booted foot caught him on the shin, and numbing pain jarred redly along his leg and up into his body. His fingers felt for the gun in his pocket, but even as they closed around it, he realised that he couldn't use it. If everything was to go according to plan, he needed this man alive.

The blow came again, smashing down against his leg. His attacker was shouting something loudly at the top of his voice, the words unintelligible. His face was a leering, grinning mask of blurred whiteness hovering above his own.

'I'll be damned if yer goin' to leave here wi' the secret . . . or try it on me.'

Slowly, the words penetrated into Peterson's consciousness. With a desperate effort, he pushed himself to his feet and heaved his body upright. He reached out, grabbing Horst's coat, heaving him close, aiming a blow. Again a fist caught him, knocking him backward.

Stumbling, stunned almost, he swayed on his feet, hitting out more by instinct than good judgement. Wildly, he shook his head to clear his fogged senses. Savagely, he tightened his hold on the old Dutchman's arm, pulling him round. His own bunched fist lashed out and caught the other full on the chin, knocking him sprawling to the floor.

Horst's face loosened. An expression of dazed surprise spread slowly over it. His eyes were glazed as he sank down onto his knees, then toppled slowly forward onto his face, his legs doubled up beneath him.

For a moment Peterson stood quite

still, staring down at the inert body of the old hillbilly. Then, pulling the body upright, he propped him up in the chair. A little pulse was throbbing painfully at the base of his throat and he was breathing heavily with the exertion. A thin trickle of blood ran down his cheek from the deep cut above his eye. He dabbed at it ineffectually. His mind felt unnaturally stiff, but cold and clear. Outside, in the pine forest, there was a graveyard silence. Nothing moved, and only the soft *shush* of his feet through the dead leaves disturbed the quietude. He walked forward quickly, seeking the place where Horst had been before. There had to be no mistakes.

Little ideas shuttled back and forth like live things in his mind, nibbling at the edges of his brain. His teeth chattered briefly in his mouth until he forced himself to relax.

That drug he had administered ought to keep the old man unconscious for close on a couple of hours, which would give him plenty of time. He felt his feet lurch and bump over loose stones, hidden beneath the climbing moss and tangled undergrowth that threatened to trip him at every turn. Thorny branches clawed at his arms. Upthrusting roots probed beneath his feet with every step. Then he was in the small clearing. Taking out his knife, he cut off a couple of small branches and placed them carefully in his pocket.

Sweat popped out on his forehead as he made his way hurriedly back to the cabin. The thin plume of blue smoke was still curling up from the single chimney. As far as he could see, in all directions the surrounding countryside was completely deserted. But in spite of that, he had the feel of eyes watching him closely from amongst the tree roots and the leafless branches. He shivered again, convulsively. It just didn't make sense, this peculiar tingling of fear that seemed to be continually running through him.

Going up to the heavy wooden door, he pushed it open and went inside. The unconscious body of Horst still lay propped in the tall chair, his chest rising and falling slowly, the only indication that he was still alive.

Slowly, the trembling inside Peterson's body ceased. A moment later, he found the length of long black twine which the other had used to fasten the two branches together in the form of a cross.

Peterson felt his muscles stiffen as he stood up with the crude cross in his left hand. Almost automatically, his fingers tensed until they dug deep into his palms. Even though this time he knew exactly what to do and what to expect, the knowledge of what was to come sent an unpleasant thrill through him. The small hairs on the back of his neck began to prickle uncomfortably. His throat felt suddenly dry, and he went over to the table and poured himself another shot of homemade liquor, drinking it down in a single gulp. It stung his palette, burning his throat, but brought some of the warmth back into his body.

Taking out his knife, he drew the sharp blade carefully along Horst's arm, just above the wrist, holding the limp hand so that the blood dripped onto the wooden cross. Now it was done. Seconds ticked past. Swaying slightly, Peterson bent over the cross on the floor at his feet and began to chant the curse he had memorised.

The words seemed to come naturally to his lips, as though he had used them many times before. He could feel a coldness at the back of his neck as he recited them, and there seemed to be an odour of death and decay around him in the room, like some great animal was poised there, invisible, lurking in the shadows.

Out of the corner of his eye, he thought he saw something move, but when he turned his head there was nothing. Whatever it had been, it was no longer there, and he fought down the rising tide of panic in his chest. After all, didn't he now know the hex? Very soon, if this worked, he would be all-powerful, able to kill men at a distance. Then he would show everyone back home. No longer would they be able to scoff and laugh at his ideas. For couldn't he now bring them back proof of what he had been saying all along?

For a moment, after he had finished, he

stood there, scarcely able to move a single muscle. Had he remembered everything? Was there some little detail he had forgotten? A hundred possibilities flashed through his mind as he looked down at the tiny wooden cross and then across the room at Horst.

Patiently, he fastened the cross onto a piece of black thread and let it dangle from the low rafters. It swung gently to and fro in the room, the blood standing out blackly where it had soaked into the wood. The cross seemed to be covered with it.

A sudden chill came over Peterson, not so much from the coldness of the air inside the room as from something subtle that caught at his nerves. He turned his head and tried to shut out the low keening murmur of the wind outside, which was like some wild, lost creature trying to get in. Somehow there seemed to be a voice in it that gave him a sick, sinking feeling in the pit of his stomach. It was an empty voice, lonely and vast and far away. He shivered. A voice that spoke of death; a screaming of torture; a last gasping, frenzied breath; of hell itself.

'There's nothing there,' Peterson muttered to himself after a moment's pause. He watched the wooden cross, but nothing had happened. It still swung there gently as though mocking him, defying him to do his worst.

What if the old man had been telling the truth? Was it possible that the hex wouldn't work on a human being, but only on animals? It seemed strange that he hadn't found any reference to it during his research into the old legends that had prompted all of this.

He cocked his head a little to one side, listening. The sudden sound behind him caused him to look round in sudden alarm, his hand diving for the revolver in his pocket. He had it half-drawn, pointing, when he saw that it was only Horst who had regained consciousness.

'So you've finally come round, eh?' said Peterson slowly. He put the gun away. 'Well, at least you'll be awake when the curse takes effect.'

Horst shook his head slowly, not comprehending.

Peterson got up and stood over him, looking down, and there was no trace of pity in his eyes. 'I thought you might like to see some of my handiwork,' he said harshly. 'See — the cross, hanging from the beam. Your cross. I performed the hex especially for you.'

The other's mouth dropped slightly open as the full realisation came to him. Fear sprang unbidden into his eyes, and he seemed on the point of leaping forward, out of the chair. Then he seemed to think better of it, and sank back, gasping. 'So that was what ye really wanted?' he said softly. 'To use the hex to kill a man.'

Peterson smiled thinly. 'In a way, yes. But don't you realise what this means? I can kill a man and get away with it. The law can't touch me, because as far as it's concerned, such things as *hexerei* don't exist. You can't send a man to prison simply for willing another dead, or for dabbling in a little mumbo-jumbo. Nobody would convict me on that evidence.' He laughed shrilly and went over to the window, looking out. 'Haven't you got anything to say?' he asked tauntingly. 'Any last wish you want to make?'

'I've nothin' to say,' said Horst stubbornly, without looking up. He seemed resigned to the fact that he would soon be dead.

Peterson turned away from the window and walked back into the middle of the room. Deep down inside, he was savouring every moment of the situation. It gave him the feeling of power he had always desired; to know that this man here would die soon, and just as surely as if you were to shoot him or throw him off the mountaintop.

'Don't you think it's strangely ironic to be sitting here watching your fate swinging by a thread in the middle of this room?' Peterson poured himself another drink and offered one to the Dutchman, but he shook his head. He seemed to be deliberating within himself, and for one moment Peterson had the impression that Horst might be able to foil him, even at this last moment.

He went back mentally over all that

Horst had told him during the earlier demonstration. What was that point he had made about saving someone from the hex? There was nothing anyone could do. Once the cross had burnt itself out in flame. Yes, that was it.

Horst was getting up from his seat, coming forward.

'Where do you think you're going?' Peterson asked harshly. For the first time, little fingers of doubt were tugging at his brain. Did the old fool still have something up his sleeve? No, that was impossible. He himself had already seen what had happened to the chicken out there in the yard. Only a few moments earlier, from the window, he had seen it still there, lying stiff on the ground, still tied to the small wooden stake.

'I don't intend to stay here and allow ye to get away with this. Ye'll never really know whether the hex has worked or not if ye can't find ma body, will you?'

'Come back here, you old fool.' Wildly, Peterson tugged at the revolver in the pocket of his jacket.

With a surprising speed, Horst ran for

the door, pulled it open, and ran out into the yard. Madly, Peterson followed. He had the gun now, but Horst was already disappearing into the trees. Bringing up the revolver, he fired twice. The running figure staggered, fell forward in the undergrowth, straightened, and then fell.

Peterson dashed over. Going down on one knee, he felt for a pulse. There was nothing. Slowly he got to his feet, the gun hanging limply by his side. Now, as Horst had said, he would never know whether the hex really worked. He had killed this man before he could find out. And somehow he would have to get rid of the body. The man at the petrol station twenty miles or so back along the mountain road would undoubtedly remember him, and it wouldn't be long before he talked to the police about the city man who had been asking for the whereabouts of certain mountain people.

There seemed to be nothing else in the whole world except the body of the dead man at Peterson's feet and the knowledge that even in death he had defeated him, cheating him of the one thing he had desired. Somehow he managed to keep his thoughts straight.

There had to be something he could do. If only the old fool hadn't taken it into his head to run off like that, everything would have worked itself out all right. He thought about the cross hanging from the beam in the cabin. There was a sudden, biting sense of alarm in his brain that he couldn't quite define. It was almost as though something was happening somewhere else, something he ought to know about. He paused, listening. Everything was quiet. Not even a bird cry came from among the pines. Nothing seemed to move.

He had to do something, and quickly. His mind was now floundering desperately within such a morass of thoughts and half-formed ideas that he didn't know what to do for the best. He felt tired and utterly bewildered. Swaying slightly, he closed his eyes and tried to think logically. There was no sense in panicking. There had to be a way out of this somewhere if he could only see it.

After all, there was plenty of time in

which to do something. There had been no other places along the road so far as he had been able to see on his way here, and it was unlikely that the old man would have many visitors. He had only to get rid of the body, go back to his car, turn around while it was still light, and head back to the main road. He could be out of the state long before morning, and nobody would be any the wiser.

As for that idiotic cross hanging up in the kitchen of the shack, nobody would ever associate it with him. He paused as another thought struck him — maybe the hex had worked after all. The old farmer had died, and the hex didn't specify the cause.

A cold finger of ice was tracing a crazy pattern up and down Peterson's shoulder blades as he made his way slowly back to the cabin. For a moment he stood on the threshold, not daring to cross it, afraid of what he might see. Then, plucking up his courage, he went inside.

The room was dark, and it was several moments before he could accustom his eyes to the gloom. Walking over to the rafter, he gazed up at the cross swinging back and forth on the almost invisible length of thread. It was unchanged. He could even see the dark specks of blood staining the wood, mocking him evilly.

So that was that. The old man's tale had been nothing more than a concoction of lies, just like the others. He sat down in the chair and poured himself another glass of syrupy alcohol. Sipping it slowly, he forced himself to think back. It had appeared to work all right with the chicken, so why not with the man? Maybe he'd forgotten something when he had worked the hex. Something wrong in the chant, perhaps? He tried to go over it word for word, as he had heard the old Dutchman intone it precisely. No, there was nothing wrong there. He had recited it perfectly, of that he was certain.

The cross. Had he made that correctly? He knit his brows in puzzled concentration. As far as he could remember, he had done everything in an identical manner. Then where had he gone wrong? Had all this been done on purpose to make him look a fool? Had Horst known all along why he was there and deliberately arranged everything for his benefit? He had said himself that there had been others.

Yes, that could be it. Somehow the old man had poisoned that chicken out there in the yard so that it had died while he was chanting his weird curse over the cross. Angrily, Peterson slapped his clenched fist into the palm of his other hand. Fooled all the way along the line. But how had the other known of his coming?

Yes, that was it — no doubt he had been told by some of the neighbouring mountainfolk that there was a crazy city slicker wandering around the vicinity, looking for information on the *hexerei*. So why not put on such a show for his benefit, probably making himself richer by a couple of hundred dollars — and all for a pack of lies?

Peterson's anger threatened to choke him. Once more, he had been made a fool of. He was suddenly glad that he had shot the old hillbilly — one less to question in the future. Now all he had to do was remain calm. He could be out of this accursed place in an hour or so if he didn't panic.

He dabbed at the blood on his cheek. Some of it came onto the back of his hand. The cut over his eye where the other had scratched him was still bleeding. During the excitement he had forgotten about it. He walked over to the small washbasin in the corner of the room. There was a pail of cold mountain water in a stone jug and he splashed it onto his face, wiping it off with his handkerchief.

After that, he felt better. Walking back, the cross brushed against his face, and he stepped back with an oath before he realised what it was. Angrily, he brushed it away.

There was a tantalising little idea nibbling at the corner of his mind, but it refused to come out into the open so that he could recognise it; and deep down inside he had the unshakeable impression that it was something important, vitally important, which he had overlooked in his hurry.

The scratch on his forehead was beginning to throb now, and . . .

His thoughts gelled inside his head. Quite suddenly, he knew what it was. He knew now why the hex hadn't worked, while the cross still remained unchanged, swinging gently from the beam, even though the old man was already dead.

When he had bent over the cross, reciting that eldritch chant, hexing the old man who lay drugged in the chair, some of the blood from his own forehead must have fallen on the cross. The old Dutchman had been released from the hex. *It was he himself who was going to die!*

Madly, Peterson glanced about. Was it his own imagination, or were those black, discoloured stains on the wood beginning to glow? Wildly, he snatched the cross down from the beam, snapping the black thread. The wood felt oddly warm in his hands, almost as though it were alive.

What to do now? Was there anything he *could* do? He felt an odd twitching in his limbs and there seemed to be a fire in his body. He tried to think. Sweat dripped from his forehead. Some ran into his eyes, causing them to sting.

There must be a way out of this damnable mess, his mind shrieked. Horst had been released from the hex by Peterson's own blood falling on the cross. He tried to think along those lines, pushing the idea to its logical conclusion.

Therefore, all he had to do was to spill someone's or something else's blood on the cross before it burned away and he would be safe. With a wild cry, he leapt for the door. A group of clucking hens scattered at his sudden appearance and squawked away in the undergrowth. Madly, he lunged for one, feeling his fingers grasp feathers. Then the chicken slipped away and ran, long-legged, under the outhouse some ten yards away.

Fear was bubbling in Peterson's throat as he ran around the corner of the house, his eyes staring from his head. There had to be something alive around the place. Surely the old fool didn't live out here, all by himself, with only a handful of chickens? Suddenly he remembered the mongrel. Where the hell was that damnable mutt now?

Insanely, he stumbled to the front entrance, shoving the door wide. The cross dropped from his fingers, but he picked it up. Desperately, he forced his flagging muscles to respond. His heart was hammering against his ribs as though it must surely burst with the strain. There was a sharp, stabbing pain in the bottom of his lungs, and it was becoming difficult to breathe properly. A red haze danced and swayed in front of his stultified vision.

Sitting in the dirt, ten yards away, he could see the miserable dog. He stepped outside, took a couple of floundering steps, then tripped over the steps and fell forward onto his face. The wooden cross fell from his fingers and dropped onto the hard ground a couple of feet in front of him.

For a long moment Peterson lay still, panting with the exertion. The bottom of his body seemed to be suddenly numb. He tried to move his legs, but they refused to respond. His chest was burning, and there was a sudden throbbing at the back of his temples that grew steadily worse with every succeeding minute. Madly, he tried to focus his eyes on the tiny wooden cross that lay in the evening sunlight almost within reach of his clutching, flexing fingers.

Even as he watched, trying to see properly, there was a little curl of smoke rising from it. The sharp stench of burning wood reached his nostrils a moment later. The last thing he saw before pain racked his body from end to end was the sudden burst of orange flame on the ground immediately in front of him.

The Voice-Stealers

*It would have been better
if they had remained confined
to myth and legend.*

Despite retaining much of its historical and architectural opulence, the palace twenty miles northwest of Jaipur in the district of Rajasthan was far off the tourist trail. Built high atop a rugged hilltop overlooking vast stretches of dusty, barren land, it had been the dwelling place for countless nobles down the centuries until the time when the Rajput kings had concluded treaties in the early nineteenth century, accepting British sovereignty in return for local autonomy and protection from the expansionist ambitions of the Maratha empire. Its fine statues, tapestries and painted murals, although fading, portrayed many elaborate scenes from this time of its troubled history, and provided a certain ambience for the banquet that was taking place in one of the grand state rooms.

Clive Mortimer Benford was one of those partaking of the sumptuous fare.

He was a well-built, extremely wealthy American who had a passion for killing exotic wildlife in the name of sport. Hunting was in his blood, and had been ever since his father had given him a longbow at the age of six and had taken him into the forested wilds, teaching him how to stalk deer and rabbits. On his eighth birthday he had been presented with his own rifle, and from that day on had gone in search of bigger and more dangerous game, namely mountain lions and bears. To him, animals were but things to stand alongside for photographs, poised over their bullet-riddled corpses or hung as trophies on the wall, or, in the case of the slices of dead camel on his plate, to eat. He began to cut up his steak.

'So just why were you kicked out of Oxford?' he asked conversationally, yet well aware that his question was bound to offend his host. There was something about the young Indian prince, whom he had only recently met, that he didn't like — a certain cunning look in his eyes; and what was more, he was convinced the feeling was mutual.

'I wouldn't say I was 'kicked out',' Prince Deepak Singh, who sat at the head of the lavishly laid-out table around which four others were seated, answered mellowly. 'Rather, we parted company. I guess Oxford wasn't yet ready for my ground-breaking discoveries. A pity, but at the end of the day it's their loss, not mine.' There was nothing in his tone of voice to imply that he had been insulted by the nature of his guest's enquiry.

'You were studying for a doctorate in genetics, if I'm not mistaken,' said Janice Carpenter in her shrill voice. She was a writer who had come out to India in the hope of finding material on mystical practices for a book she was planning. 'A fascinating subject I'm sure, but one which I'm afraid is far too scientific for me.'

'Ever since childhood I've been interested in animal evolution, in particular the manner in which some animals and plant forms survive and flourish while others become extinct,' Singh said. 'This is often due to their inability to adapt to their environment, in addition to the

189

damaging role that man has played in their survival, by which I mean habitat alteration, industrialisation and hunting.' He smiled and nodded at Benford, whom he knew had come to India for the sole purpose of shooting game. 'For my dissertation, I collected material on a wide range of recently extinct fauna: the Javan rhinoceros, the Bali tiger, the quagga, the thylacine, and of course the much better-known dodo. However, my particular interest lies in the field of cross-species hybridisation.' He raised a hand and clicked his fingers. 'More wine.' His instructions given, two servants immediately came forward, filling glasses.

'Hybridisation? I assume that you're talking about the recent successes in breeding certain of the panthera strains?' Professor Hans Kugelbeck asked in his accented English as he dabbed at the corners of his mouth with a napkin. He was an archaeologist in his late sixties and had recently arrived from Munich with the intention of working on certain Harappan sites on the Pakistan border.

Singh nodded. 'The genetic creation of

the tigon and the liger are but two examples, but there are many more. One day — '

'Did you say tigon?' Benford interrupted. 'And what the hell's a liger? I've never heard of them, and I've spent my entire life tracking down all manner of creatures.'

'Pardon me.' Singh gave Kugelbeck an apologetic smile before turning to face the brash American. 'The tigon is the offspring of a tiger and a lioness. The liger is in some ways its mirror image, resulting from the mating of a lion and a tigress. I used to have a liger in my private menagerie. A truly incredible creature. The largest of the big cats. There is also the litigon, which is the offshoot of the lion and the female tigon, but — '

'Are these things for real?' asked Benford. If so, he wanted to know where he could go out and hunt them — although that was a question which, given the current company, he didn't ask. Hopefully he'd have a chance to find out later.

'Very much so. As I told you, I used to

own a liger. Unfortunately there was an inherent weakness in the genetic strain, and she aged faster than was natural. In the end, there was nothing any of my highly skilled veterinary staff could do.' Singh got to his feet. A small man, resplendent in his black formal suit and a turquoise silk turban, he looked much younger than his thirty-three years. 'Now, there is still much for me to do, but as my guests feel free to wander the palace. In the morning it is my wish that you all accompany me to see for yourselves some of the important work that I am currently overseeing. As some of you may know, my father ran a very successful stud farm, breeding some of the best horses in India, if not the world. Some were even sent to the polo grounds at Mumbai. I have gone much further, taking cross-species experimentation and selective breeding to levels hitherto unguessed at, advancing his work in ways that he would never have imagined.'

★   ★   ★

There was an unpleasant, queasy feeling in Benford's stomach as he sat staring out at the desolate landscape from inside the decrepit, wheezing bus. From the occasional groan from his fellow passengers, he could tell that he wasn't the only one suffering. In all probability the meal last night hadn't fully agreed with them. To make matters worse, the conditions inside the bus were far from comfortable. Even with the windows down, the heat was stifling, and from where he sat he felt as though he was getting slowly cooked from the magnified rays of the sun. Only Singh, who sat next to the driver, seemed unaffected.

The road the bus bumped and rattled along wound its way into the Rajasthan badlands. There were no villages or towns, only mile after mile of arid countryside, the sun-bleached uniformity broken only by an infrequent ruin.

There came a tap on Benford's shoulder. He turned in his seat.

'Excuse me, my good man, but am I correct in assuming that you came out here to hunt animals?' asked a thin-faced chinless man in an English upper-class voice. He had introduced himself as Sir Reginald Ashmole when they had first got on the bus.

'Sure did,' Benford drawled. 'Why d'ya ask?'

Ashmole lowered his voice until it became an almost conspiratorial whisper. 'I may be able to assist you in your endeavour. You see, I know a man in Delhi who operates safaris with the more discerning customer in mind. For a suitable sum, he's not averse to procuring certain of the more, shall we say, hard to find game.'

'Sounds interesting. Maybe — ' Benford stopped as, with a sudden lurch, the bus came to a standstill.

Singh was on his feet. 'Apologies for the bone-shaking journey, but I'm pleased to inform you that we've now arrived. Now, just a few short words about the facility before we disembark. There are basically two separate compounds. The first one we'll visit is what I refer to as the zoo. It is here that most of the animals are housed and fed. In the second area are

194

the laboratories, where much of the actual genetic work is done. This facility is also home to the veterinary hospital.'

Janice raised a hand and then asked: 'Don't you think it's fundamentally against nature to be experimenting on these creatures in such a way?'

Singh smiled. 'Against nature? Who's to say what precisely nature is? If man has the capability of creating a new strain of life through biological fusion, then I see no ethical dilemma. Here in India we have a code of ethics when it comes to vivisection that is quite probably more stringent than those in most Western countries. I can assure you that nothing is done here which breaches any laws. To me, the welfare of my animals is paramount. Well, if we're all ready, I see no reason not to start the tour.' He turned his back on the others and leapt down from the bus.

Benford privately doubted much of what the prince had said. Nevertheless he followed, relieved to be no longer suffering the dreadful motion sickness that had plagued him for the past forty minutes. Shading his eyes against the terrible brightness, he could see a collection of single-storey buildings surrounded by a barbed-wire fence. There was an overall drabness about the place; and a thick, cloying stench that reminded him of his uncle's pig farm back in Kansas polluted the air. There was also a hellish screeching coming from over to his right, and peering in that direction he could see, beyond the outer fence, a crude cage in which frenetic shapes, probably monkeys, leapt and scurried.

Once his four guests were off the bus, Singh began walking to a small sentry box that stood at the side of the main gate. Inside was a guard, a rifle slung over his shoulder. Belching noisome exhaust fumes and throwing up a great cloud of dust, the bus pulled away.

Benford appraised the man with the rifle. Admittedly, savage animals were kept here; but it wasn't as though there was any threat to the public, for the installation was miles from anywhere and he doubted whether it ever got any casual visitors. Even if several of the lions or tigers did manage to escape, he doubted whether they'd get far in this sweltering heat and with no water for miles around. From past experience, he knew that creatures which had been bred in captivity became soft, unable to fully revert back to surviving in the wild where meals weren't delivered at set times and where competition was fierce. Some became docile, almost domestic, dependent on humans for their existence.

Singh conversed with the guard in his own dialect. Moments later the gate was opened, and, ushering his guests forward, he led them towards a large wooden barn-like structure. The horrendous stench became more overpowering.

'Please forgive the smell,' commented Singh. 'This building we're now approaching houses the various pens in which some of the animals are kept. In addition there are a few cages, mostly for the primates and the big cats, over on the far side of the complex, which we may have the opportunity of visiting later.' He gave a nonchalant wave of his hand to two men who came out of a large side door carrying buckets. 'We're in luck. It appears that we've arrived at feeding time. I must ask you all to be cautious around the animals, both for your sake and for theirs.'

The five of them entered the building. As Benford had suspected, the area inside resembled huge stables, divided into numerous stalls and pens with a central walkway down the middle. The noise inside was a chaotic cacophony of screeches, barks, yelps and roars, which seemed to tear at his brain as assuredly as the claws of the strange-looking badger-like creatures he was currently looking down at.

Kugelbeck leaned over the side and then quickly drew his hand away as one of the vicious animals sprang for him. 'What are these?' he asked, turning to Singh.

'These are Rajasthan desert badgers. They're unique to this vicinity and are native to the foothills south of here. They are very aggressive, and unlike badgers found elsewhere in the world, they are purely carnivorous. Let me show you.'

Singh removed a thick chainmail gauntlet that hung on a hook nearby and put it on. There was a bucket filled with meat scraps at the door to the pen and he took out a large chunk, which he then dangled over the side.

The effect was startling. The closest three badgers ceased snuffling about and made frenzied leaps at the meat. Two latched on with their razor-sharp teeth and dragged it from Singh's hand. There followed a violent battle on the ground as all six of them then fought over the meat, tearing it to pieces and devouring it in a show of terrible raptorial hunger.

It reminded Benford of something he had once read about a school of piranhas stripping an elephant to the bone in no time at all. 'Hell, they sure were hungry,' he said.

'They always are,' replied Singh. 'It is most unfortunate, but if they're not fed regularly they are known to turn cannibalistic. Consequently, in the wild they tend to be solitary creatures. Here, part of my research is concerned with trying to breed this compulsive hunger from them;

to make them more sociable and — '

'What the hell's this?' asked Benford. He had wandered over to a pen on the other side, away from the badgers. The long, lizard-like creature he was looking at had a hardened shell on its back like that of a tortoise; but its profile, to say nothing of its angular, snouted jaws, was more like that of a crocodile. There didn't appear to be any movement from it in the slightest, leading him to the conclusion that it was either fast asleep or dead.

Singh sauntered over. 'That is a mutant, a freak which I obtained from a North African trader. Preliminary tests have shown that its genetic makeup is part freshwater crocodile and part turtle. I believe it to be a true quirk of nature. A real one-off.'

'A most peculiar animal,' commented Ashmole.

Benford had already passed on to the next holding area. This one housed five piebald pygmy horses, no larger than medium-sized dogs. Whilst unusual, they held no real interest for him, and he quickly walked on. Here was a large tank filled with dark water in which initially he could see nothing. Then, just as he was about to call to Singh to ask if there was anything inside, the surface rippled and two serpent heads reared before him, their twin forked tongues flicking the air. Hastily, he pulled well back.

'Please be careful!' warned Singh, rushing over.

Now that the initial shock had worn off, Benford tried to compose himself. It was only a couple of snakes after all, and he had killed hundreds over the years. Both heads sank into the murky water once more. 'I didn't recognise either of them from their markings. What were they?'

'They? That was one creature. A genuine amphisbaena.'

'A what?'

'It is a two-headed snake. The product of successful genetic engineering.' Singh guided Benford away from the tank. 'For centuries they were considered extinct; monsters of myth and legend. Through a specialised breeding program I have restored life to a species on which nature had turned her back. Further work is needed on establishing in which habitat these creatures will thrive, but it is my ambition to be able to release all of them to the wild one day.' He was going to say more when a somewhat nervous-looking technician came walking briskly forward and muttered something in an Indian language into his ear.

Despite not knowing what was communicated, it was obvious to Benford that something was wrong. Some of the colour bleached from Singh's face. Gulping, he turned to his guests.

'I'm afraid there's been a slight problem. If I can just ask you all to follow me outside.' Hurriedly, using an exit at the other end of the building, he ushered everyone out of the building.

'What's wrong?' asked Benford.

'It's nothing to worry about,' said Singh. 'Just a slight problem.' He spoke again with the technician. After a few moments, he then dispatched the other to the security guard at the gate. Then he turned to those assembled. 'If you'd all just remain here while I go and find out what's wrong. I assure you it's nothing to panic about.' The guard with the rifle rushed over. 'Please, wait here.' Snatching the rifle from his hands, Singh and the other then dashed over to a squat grey building built from breeze-blocks.

Benford took in the confused faces of his fellow visitors, noting the concerned looks.

'What do you think's the matter?' asked Janice. It was clear she was trying to conceal her fear.

'Hard to say,' answered Benford. 'Could be anything. Something to do with the electrics or the water supply. Maybe they've had an infestation of roaches.'

'Or something's got out.'

All eyes turned to Ashmole.

The Englishman shrugged his narrow shoulders. 'Well, it's possible, is it not? I had a friend who used to work at Windsor Safari Park, and he once told me how a tiger had managed to escape from its cage. By the time they'd succeeded in getting it back, it had mauled its — '

There came a loud gunshot that caused

everyone but Benford to jump.

'Good God!' exclaimed Ashmole, looking in the direction from which the sound had come with wide, staring eyes.

'That was a gun, wasn't it?' asked Janice.

'Sure was.' Benford took a few steps forward. Apart from themselves, there was no one else around. The door to the building which Singh had entered hung open, and he expected the young prince to come out having now taken care of the 'problem'. It seemed that an animal had escaped after all.

A minute passed, and no one emerged. There was a tightness in Benford's stomach; a tensing of muscles. His eyes narrowed as he stared at the doorway some sixty yards away. Another minute passed, and he could now feel a tingling sensation in his hands. If something had broken free of its cage, then surely it had been shot and was now dead. So where the hell were Singh and the gate guard?

'Do you think they're all right?' asked Janice nervously.

'Perhaps one of us should go and see,'

suggested Ashmole, looking pointedly at Benford. It was abundantly clear that he didn't feel up to the task.

'Yes, maybe that would be for the best,' seconded Kugelbeck. 'Just to make sure that nothing untoward has happened.'

'Be my guest,' said Benford. Had he a gun in his hand, he would have been the first to go and investigate; but unarmed, he didn't relish coming face to face with whatever creatures might be inside. Given the bizarre nature of the animals he had seen so far, it could be just about anything.

'Well, I . . . ' Kugelbeck faltered. Mumbling darkly to himself, he mustered his courage, and his face hardened. 'Very well.'

Benford felt a stab of guilt. He cursed his own cowardice. 'Hold up there! I'll come along with you,' he said.

Together the two of them headed for the door. A wind blew up, gusting dust into mini-whirlwinds and causing the door to slam against the outer wall. The riotous screeching from the creatures in the stables behind them died down and a portentous silence fell over them, broken only by the banging of the door.

'I don't know what's going on, but things aren't looking too good,' commented Benford. Tentatively he edged towards the door, preparing himself to act without a moment's hesitation, his nerves coiled like a cobra about to strike. His nostrils twitched as an unpleasant odour wafted out from inside. It was very different from the animal stench he had come to associate with this place; more like vomit mixed with carrion that had been left to rot in the desert sun.

'Eugh!' mumbled Kugelbeck, pinching his nose. 'That's terrible. What is it?'

'Christ knows.' Switching seamlessly into stalking mode, Benford stealthily went inside. The small room was drab, and what furniture was there was basic and utilitarian. Directly opposite from where he stood there was another door, which was also wide open. Beyond, he could see a stretch of corridor lit by intermittently flickering fluorescent strip lights.

'Anything?' asked Kugelbeck.

'Nope.' Benford halted. He wasn't sure, but he thought he could hear voices coming from the far end of the corridor, where he could make out the entrance to a dark and shadow-filled room twenty or so yards away. The continual flashing of the lights was proving hard on the eyes. 'Say, is everything all right?' he called out.

With a sudden abruptness, the voices stopped.

'Singh!'

Silence.

'Singh!' Benford called out a second time, louder, his shout echoing down the passage. When there was no reply, he turned to Kugelbeck and shrugged his shoulders. The perplexity on the German archaeologist's face mirrored that on his own. 'I could have sworn I heard someone down there.'

'Maybe we should head back,' suggested Kugelbeck.

'I'll be damned if I will.' Ignoring the other's advice, Benford stepped out into the corridor. 'Singh! Quit fooling around, will you?'

For a long moment there was silence

— an eerie silence. Then came a sound, low and hushed: a mewling screech that came from nothing and warped into a man's voice. The words were in an Indian dialect, but Benford was in no doubt that it was Singh speaking.

An abominable horror slinked from the shadows.

At first Benford thought it was some kind of horse or a large deer, but as it came closer he saw that it had a shaggy mane like a lion's and a head like one of those voracious badgers he had seen minutes ago. Its maw, however, was different. Gone was the snapping, razor-edged teeth. Instead, its mouth was more like a serrated, bony ridge; bladed and scissor-like — ideal for shearing away limbs. It was unlike anything he had seen before: a truly detestable composite chimera — an unholy mismatch of stag, lion and badger. There was an almost Pleistocene look to it.

'God help us!' cried Kugelbeck.

'What the hell is it?' asked Benford, not taking his eyes from the creature as it stalked forward, illuminated disturbingly in the flashing light. There was an unholiness about it; an almost palpable aura of evil which, accompanied by the horrendous stink, made his skin crawl.

'A leucrotta,' the professor gasped in horror.

Benford had never heard of such a beast. Unarmed as he was, he knew he had no chance of tackling it. One snap from those jaws or one hefty kick from a hoof would spell disaster. Grabbing Kugelbeck by the arm, he dragged him back. Soon they were outside in the blazing heat and sunlight.

'Close the door and barricade it!' ordered the German.

'With what?' asked Benford. A pleading voice he was certain was Singh's echoed from inside.

'Come on! We must get away from this place. My God, what madness drove him to create such foul beings?' Kugelbeck's eyes, wide and filled with terror, were focused on the doorway.

'What about Singh? We can't just — '

'He's already dead. According to legend, the leucrotta's capable of stealing the voice of those it kills.'

'What?' There was stark incredulity on Benford's face.

'Is anything the matter?' hollered Ashmole, coming towards them.

Benford turned to face the Englishman. He was about to reply when, in a dark flash, the monstrous quadruped sprang out, galloping swiftly toward them. Rearing up on its hind legs, it bore down on Kugelbeck, battering him to the dusty ground.

The attack on the German archaeologist was terrible. The thing he had called a leucrotta raised its hooves, bringing them down, savagely trampling its victim, pounding the now soggy remains, reducing the man to a bloody, flattened, leaking paste.

Benford had witnessed animal ferocity before, several times. Three years ago his brother, a fellow hunting enthusiast, had been gored to death by a bull elephant whilst on safari in Kenya. He had seen a friend ambushed and savaged by a leopard in Tanzania, and another torn apart by a grizzly bear in Canada, but this was worse, far worse. The fury of the attack went beyond mere animal predation. There was a malign glint in the thing's eyes, almost as though this hellish fiend was taking delight in what it was doing. Whatever these biological throwbacks were, it seemed that they were perfect killing machines; and what was more, they enjoyed killing.

'Oh my God!' mouthed Ashmole, his face aghast at the sickening violence.

Spattered in the German's blood, the evil ungulate made a sudden lunge and tore away Kugelbeck's throat, swallowing the vocal apparatus — the larynx, pharynx, trachea and tongue — in one greedy gobble. It turned to face the shocked Englishman.

'Where's the hell's Singh with his gun?' Ashmole screamed.

'He's already dead.' The words, spoken perfectly in Kugelbeck's voice, came from the dreadful bony-ridged, gore-spattered muzzle of the hideous beast.

'Jesus Christ! It's true! It speaks!' Insanity came crashing down on Benford as his mind reeled. This was utter madness, a nightmare. Shaking, he staggered back.

There came a sudden high-pitched scream from Janice.

Benford spun round. To his absolute horror, he saw a second leucrotta come trotting out from around the rear of the building. The creature tilted its head to one side, sniffing the air, picking up the scent of its prey. A babbling gibberish, spoken in an Indian language, poured from its mouth. The beast that had killed Kugelbeck, and presumably Singh, began to edge towards Ashmole.

As a hunter, Benford knew most of the strategies and techniques by which animals hunted their prey. He knew that lions would intentionally target the young and the infirm, and that wolves would operate in packs to bring down larger creatures, possessing a high degree of social intelligence. However, in the eyes of these monsters he could see a depraved cunning that went far beyond this. Right now, he knew that of the three of them — himself, Ashmole and Janice — only one of them stood any chance of getting away. There were two leucrottas, and if they were each to make a run for it in different directions . . .

As though they had read his mind, Ashmole and Janice turned and fled. The leucrottas gave immediate chase.

Knowing that he had to seize the opportunity, Benford spun round and began to run. Heart pounding, he sprinted for a slightly more modern-looking building which he assumed was the laboratory Singh had mentioned. In his ears he could hear bloodcurdling screams from the other two, but not once did he look back. This was a question of survival, and he knew that to slow down or hesitate would assuredly mean death.

He was nearing a door. Hands outstretched, he made a lunge for it, hoping that it wouldn't be locked. Mercifully it flew open, and he stumbled into a laboratory. Two long wooden benches, atop which were microscopes, centrifuges, incubators, and a wide range of other pieces of scientific apparatus he didn't recognise, ran down either side of the room. Over to his right stood a fume cupboard, near to which was another door. A pungent, vinegary stink hung in the air, visible as a brownish-grey haze near the ceiling.

Risking a quick backward glance, Benford saw no signs of movement. Apart from Kugelbeck's mangled corpse, there was nothing untoward; no trace of the leucrottas or the two who had fled from them. He could only hope that they had somehow reached safety.

He pulled the door to. What he needed right now was a weapon and some ammunition; preferably a high-powered rifle and a box filled with the kind of bullets that would blast those horrors to hell and back. His spirits rose slightly at the thought of bagging one of them and displaying its head on the wall of his New York State hunting lodge.

However, there were no guns here; and as far as he knew, the only one lay back somewhere in that other building — not that it had been of much use to Singh. Benford crossed to the other door and turned the handle. Beyond was a second laboratory. Two more doors, one to his left and one straight in front, permitted access to other areas.

Grabbing a chair, he wedged it tightly against the door. He doubted whether it would stand up to a forceful kick from a leucrotta, but it was better than nothing. Now that he was out of any immediate danger, he found it curious that there weren't any more staff around. So far he had only seen the gate guard, one technician, and the two men who had delivered the meat and the slops. It seemed inconceivable that there was no one else . . . unless, of course, they were now dead. He tried not to dwell on that thought, for it gave rise to darker possibilities, such as the likelihood that there were more than two of those man-killers on the prowl.

Taking some deep breaths, Benford tried to calm his tortured nerves. He knew that he was once more in a life-or-death situation — something he thrived on when he was the one in charge; the one with the gun. Now, however, with the realisation that the hunter had become the hunted, he felt a surge of fear deep inside. He knew that those monsters were highly intelligent and that they could be anywhere, lurking in readiness to ambush him from the shadows. Gripping his hair, he tried to force himself to think rationally — cold and logically, to try and detach himself emotionally from what was happening. He knew that was the only way to stave off madness and survive this experience. To succumb to the fear would almost certainly prove fatal.

Opening one of the doors, he found himself at the end of a short corridor. There was nothing visible save for a mop and bucket propped against the wall halfway along. The door at the far end was open and led outside. Benford was wrestling with the idea of taking his chances outside in order to see if he could make it to the main gate when, some distance behind him, he heard a door crashing open.

'Help me! For God's sake, help me!' came a yell.

It sounded exactly like Ashmole's plummy aristocratic voice, but Benford refused to believe that it was. Slowly, he began to edge along the corridor that led out.

A sudden, shrill scream made him jump. Half-expecting to see one of the devious leucrottas at the end of the corridor, his heart leapt when he saw Janice standing in the doorway. She was looking, panic-stricken, over her shoulder.

'Quick — in here!' Benford hissed. When he saw her turn in his direction, he hastily beckoned her over. She came towards him in a mad rush.

Barely a second later, the dark shape of a leucrotta sprang into the entrance. Framed in the doorway, the monster looked utterly wicked and unnatural — a freakish creation whose sole purpose, it seemed, was to kill. It barked, then uttered a demonic whinnying sound that echoed disturbingly down the corridor.

'Oh my God!' Janice cried, covering her ears.

'Come on!' Benford grabbed her by an arm and dragged her forcibly away from the approaching terror.

There were noises coming from the

first laboratory he had entered — crashes as of some disruptive, destructive force taking the place apart. Above the wrecking could be heard sporadic outbursts of a male Indian voice shouting madly, intermingled with the mumblings of an English toff. It was a chaotic, mind-warping, glossolalic noise.

Benford looked for an escape. There was one more door he had yet to try. Rushing over, he threw it open. Beyond was a flight of narrow stone steps descending into the darkness.

'It's the only way.' Benford didn't like the idea of having to go down there, but staying where they were wasn't an option. Steadying Janice, he went down, using a hand to maintain his balance. Reaching the bottom, he was relieved to feel a light switch. He flicked it down. Instant illumination lit the small basement.

The room was filled with all manner of things — spare parts for the machines upstairs, in the main. There were also stacked animal cages, several large water containers, bits and pieces of furniture, a few old filing cabinets, and a wide array of tools heaped in a corner. There were no firearms to be seen, but there was a petrol-driven chainsaw, a wood axe, and three six-foot-long metal poles that had been sharpened at one end.

Benford's heart sank; for, aside from the way they had entered, there was no exit. 'It looks like those bastards have us,' he said, retrieving the wood axe. He peered around the corner of the wall, looking back up the stairs. Any moment now he expected one of the horrors to come into view. It was then that a small glimmer of hope sparked in his heart. The stairs were extremely narrow and almost precipitous in their ascent. Surely a horse-like creature wouldn't be able to negotiate them. He had barely managed it down, admittedly helping Janice, without tripping. Something on four legs would have no chance.

'There's no way out, is there?' mumbled Janice. It seemed her initial shock had faded and the reality of their imprisonment had registered. 'We're trapped!'

'We'll get out . . . somehow,' Benford

tried to reassure her, but his words lacked conviction.

A shadow that made his heart lurch crept across the doorway above. An elongated snout came into view — fresh blood dribbling from the saw-like ridge of the thing's mouth. A putrid stink filled the stairway as steaming, grey-black droppings fell from the leucrotta's rear end and splattered onto the floor. The voice-stealing nightmare clip-clopped cautiously towards the first step.

Sickened, Benford watched, weighing up the possibility of goading the creature forward in the hope that it would stumble and come flying down the stairs, breaking its legs — or even better, its neck. He could tell that it was considering its options.

Warily, like someone testing the temperature of a bath, the beast extended a front leg and brought it down on the uppermost step. Unsteadily, it tried to put its weight on it, pitched forward, and then managed to right itself. Pulling back, having now decided that such a risky manoeuvre was beyond it, the leucrotta retreated to the top of the stairs.

'Thank God! It looks like it can't get down the stairs.' Benford turned to Janice. 'I guess we're safe here.'

'But . . . for how long? We can't stay here forever.'

'I know.' Benford was thinking. 'Someone's bound to come out here to find out what's going on. Singh's sure to be missed. And I'd have thought that bus driver would be coming back for us. He'll get help.'

'So what do we do in the meantime?'

'I'd say there's little we can do but sit this out. There's a chance that now that those creatures know they can't get to us, they'll go elsewhere. Also, if they're related to those Rajasthan desert badgers we first saw, then when their food supply runs out they may turn on each other. If that's the case, then no doubt one will devour the other. The survivor might be sufficiently weakened for us to either kill it or evade it.' He walked over and picked up one of the sharpened metal poles. Stabbing it in the air, he decided it would make a pretty effective spear.

'I wish I'd never agreed to meet Singh in the first place,' said Janice. 'I knew I should've turned down that palace invitation.'

Benford nodded. 'You got one too, did you?'

'Yes, as did the professor.' Janice perched herself atop one of the water barrels. 'He told me how pleasantly surprised he'd been. Like me, he couldn't understand why he'd been invited. Guess we'll never know now.'

Benford had thought little of it at the time. The hand-written letter, delivered by one of the prince's messengers, had been polite and courteous, enquiring as to whether he would care to attend one of His Excellence's banquets. How could he refuse? But now, the more he thought about it, a dark, paranoid notion began to blossom in his mind. Some of the colour drained from his face and he felt his stomach muscles tighten. Was it conceivable that there was a malign motive behind Singh's invitation? Had he brought them all here with the intention of offering them to these hellspawn?

There was a pronounced variation in each of their voices: his rich American drawl; Kugelbeck's Germanic-slanted pronunciation; Ashmole's perfect, educated, well-spoken English; and Janice's high-pitched tone — a uniqueness in their speech patterns and mannerisms which would have been ideal for experimentation purposes in regard to the leucrottas. If that had been Singh's diabolical scheme, it appeared that there had been a terrible mishap, with the monsters getting out shortly before the guests had arrived. Try as he might to persuade himself otherwise, now that this theory had taken root, it was impossible to shake away.

'You look sick,' commented Janice.

Benford nodded. 'It's the smell,' he lied. The possibility that Singh had brought them out here with the intention of feeding them to the leucrottas made his blood boil. Although he hadn't seen Singh's remains, he was certain that the prince was dead, a victim of his own creations. He wouldn't have the satisfaction of killing the man himself.

There came a loud crash from directly

overhead. This was followed by a maddened hammering that caused the ceiling to shake. It was like an earthquake. Plaster snowed from the ceiling and the light flickered. In his mind's eye, Benford could envisage one of the monsters stampeding around the room above, bucking like a wild stallion. The noise lasted for several minutes.

Then a worrying silence descended, making Benford uneasy. While that hellish din had lasted, he knew where at least one of them was. Now, he had no idea. Had they both gone? Or were they waiting, trying to lure him and Janice into a false sense of security? The beasts were cunning, and he was only too aware that they possessed a level of intelligence far surpassing that of any normal animal. As a hunter himself, he knew the importance of being patient; to wait until an opportune moment presented itself. He knew that he could sit tight down here for as long as it took, but he doubted whether Janice could. How much longer could she endure a diabolical game of cat and mouse?

'They're going to kill us, aren't they?' she whimpered. 'Just like the professor and Mr Ashmole.'

'Don't talk like that!' snapped Benford. 'I've told you — we're going to get out of this. All we have to do is wait. Those monsters aren't going to stay up there forever. Maybe it would be for the best if you tried to get some sleep. Don't worry, I'll stay on watch.'

* * *

The gaping mouth stretched wider, like that of a crocodile about to chomp down on its prey. An utterly horrible exhalation blasted forth as the ridged jaws elongated further. A slimy, mottled tongue slobbered forth. The dark gullet grew in size, a black abyss from which came obscene gargling sounds. Then a shape began to appear within the bottomless pit of the throat. It was a head. Kugelbeck's battered and bloody head. The dead German's mouth opened and —

With a jerk, Benford sprang awake. It was pitch dark and he was completely unaware of his surroundings. The vestiges of the terrible nightmare still lingered in his brain, and the overwhelming sensation of disorientation caused his mind to spin. A cold sweat streaked his face and his shirt felt clammy on his back. Unable to check his wristwatch, he had no idea how long he had been asleep. It could have been minutes. It could have been hours. He could hear the rhythmic sound of someone lightly snoring.

A scream rose unbidden to his lips as realisation dawned. He had drifted off. Janice was sleeping nearby; and to make matters a hundred times worse, the lights must have fused whilst he had been out. Like a flash flood, a dark tide of uncontrollable fear flowed through Benford, freezing his blood and almost drowning him in its terror-filled embrace.

It was then that he heard the noises.

Ghastly sounds that came from somewhere in the darkness — evil whispers and unholy cries that played havoc with his mind; cruel taunts and pathetic pleas that drove an icy blade into his heart. There was a myriad of different voices

226

that seemed to come from all around, as though he were being tormented by a sadistic ventriloquist. It was an evil spell that conjured horrible images, peopling the frightening, impenetrable darkness with unspeakable demons. It was hard to tell whether the unearthly acoustics were real or whether they were mere figments of his overwrought imagination. On and on they went; an insane babble that gnawed at his mind, tearing at the very fabric of his sanity.

Yet the more he listened, the more Benford became convinced that the sounds weren't the product of his sickened imagination. There were discernible patterns in the seemingly chaotic cacophony: a subtle continuous repetition that he was able to pick out. He became certain that the leucrottas weren't capable of independent human speech, but rather they were regurgitating phrases which they no doubt had heard. Like monstrous parrots, their words and phrases were no more than an impressive display of mimicry. Such a realisation could prove useful.

Blindly, he reached to one side, his fingers tightening around the spear-like pole.

The voices stopped.

All was quiet for a very long time.

★ ★ ★

'Is anyone there? It's Dhiraj, the bus driver!'

Benford sprang up, fully alert. In the darkness it was hard to tell whether he had been sleeping or not. 'Janice! Wake up!' He stumbled over to where he knew she lay, still fast asleep. 'Get up!'

Janice stirred and began to mumble.

Benford began to shake her awake. 'The bulb must've fused. Someone's come to rescue us. We have to go.'

'It's Dhiraj, the bus driver!' came the shout again.

Benford made for the steps then stopped. *Wait a minute*, he thought. *How could I be so stupid as to be taken in by this ruse?* This ploy was just the kind of thing those canny monsters used to such lethal effect. The real bus driver was in all

228

probability nothing more than a hoof-imprinted puddle of rogan josh. However, there was one way of putting things to the test.

'What's your name and who do you work for?' he yelled, reasoning that if the answer that came back was nothing but a nonsensical regurgitation, then he would have his answer regarding the other's true identity.

'Is that you, Mr American man?' The voice was near, and a moment later the door at the top of the stairs was opened. Outlined in the rectangle of electric light was a man.

'Thank Christ!' Gripping his metal pole, Benford headed up the stairs, half-dragging Janice behind him.

'I could find no one. I was about to head back to the palace. Have you seen His Excellency?' asked the bus driver.

It was clear that although riled, the man wasn't out of his wits with fear, leading Benford to the belief that he hadn't yet seen or learnt anything of the true horrors of this place. 'Singh's dead,' he said.

'*Dead?*' Dhiraj backed away.

'Yes, dead. There was a breakout by some of his animals. Didn't you see anything unusual outside?'

Dhiraj shook his head.

'Well, let's hope the coast's clear. Come on, if we want to get out of this place alive we've to get going. There's no telling when they'll come back.' Taking Janice by the hand, Benford gestured for the bus driver to start moving. 'Now, where's your bus parked?'

'At the main gate.'

'Good!'

The three of them left the laboratory building and slipped out into the cool Rajasthan evening. Twilight was still an hour away and the sky was a dismal shade of tangerine.

Benford was on constant lookout, dreading the sudden appearance of one or both of the leucrottas. At any moment, he expected one of them to come trotting around the side of a building or to hear the terrifying sound of galloping hooves behind him. His grip on the metal pole tightened. If one of them came for him, he was determined not to go down without a fight.

Their shadows were long as they crossed the open compound. Benford knew this was when they were at their most vulnerable. He did a full circle, ensuring that there was nothing sneaking up on them. Over to one side, he could make out a revolting patch on the ground — all that now remained of the flattened Kugelbeck. It wasn't that surprising that Dhiraj hadn't noticed it, for the bulk of the professor's corpse had been dragged off elsewhere, as evidenced by a bloody trail.

They were now nearing the animal pens. The noise from within was strangely subdued, almost as though the creatures inside knew that there was something worse than them on the prowl. Up ahead, beyond the entrance gate and the guard post, Benford could see the bus.

Janice made a sudden dash for it. Turning briefly in mid-sprint, she shouted: 'We've made it!' She reached the passenger door and screamed.

From around the back of the bus

stepped one of the four-legged horrors.

'Janice!' Benford cried, running forward.

The leucrotta heard his shout and turned to face him.

It was at that moment that the second beast, which had been hiding in wait behind a large boulder on the right, sprang from its concealment. It charged Benford, its downward bite blocked by the metal pole, its jaws clamped vice-like around it.

Locked in a savage tug of war he knew he had no chance of winning, Benford was about to release the pole when to his shock and surprise the monster sheared it in half. Armed with two smaller poles, he fiercely brought both jagged-edged lengths of metal stabbing inwards, plunging one into the thing's left eye, the other into its throat. Dark crimson blood ran down his hands.

The beast went berserk. Rearing up on its hind legs, it kicked at the air. Benford staggered clear. Through glazed eyes, he saw the other horror batter Janice to the ground, catching her with a kick to the side of the body, the force of which spun her round like a whirling marionette. Then Dhiraj was screaming at the top of his voice, striking at it with his bare hands, pummelling its flank, his attack courageous but largely ineffectual.

It spun round. Snapping down, it caught the bus driver by the arm, severing it completely just above the elbow. Blood sprayed from his ragged stump as he reeled back before sinking to his knees.

'*Help!* For the love of God, help me!' That was Ashmole's voice coming from the wounded leucrotta. Next came a whining scream as the beast began to thrash around, dislodging the barb in its throat. Blood streamed from the one pinned to its eye.

Heart pounding, Benford made a run for it, heading back into the compound. The closest building was the stables. Once inside, he slammed the door shut behind him. There seemed to be no escape from this nightmare. The place stank and the noise bordered on the unbearable, but right now he was past caring. He looked around for something to defend himself with, but there was little of use here apart from — He stopped and stared at the six badgers.

Suddenly the door behind him burst open. Singh's voice cried out from the doorway. Then came Janice's high-pitched scream.

Fully aware that there was little else he could do, Benford pushed back the heavy bolt that locked the gate to the badger enclosure. He threw open the pen door and dashed for the exit on the other side.

The voracious badgers scurried out. A violent, frenzied attack on the leucrotta then ensued. It kicked and snapped at the much smaller beasts, but what they lacked in size they made up for in numbers.

To add to the chaos and to make a greater distraction, Benford released the pygmy horses, knowing full well that they would fast become snacks for the untameable predators. He watched from the doorway, eager to be away yet captivated by the fierce spectacle. Two of the badgers lay still and lifeless, but the remaining four tore savagely at the leucrotta, its flanks now covered in blood and foam. And then it was on the ground, one badger snapped in half by its powerful jaws. They then targeted the soft underbelly, burrowing into the thing's abdomen, dislodging a heap of glistening entrails. Driven by an insatiable blood-lust, the badgers continued to bite and claw.

Benford had seen more than enough. He felt sick, yet he knew now was his best chance of escape. He dashed back to the bus, aware that the leucrotta he had wounded earlier was still out there somewhere.

It was getting dark. Janice was dead. Dhiraj was dead. Everyone but himself who had come to this accursed place was dead.

Searching the bus driver's one-armed corpse, he soon found the keys to the bus. Wearily, he opened the door and clambered inside. He sat down in the driver's seat and started the engine. Throwing on the lights, he saw the wounded leucrotta lying sprawled in the road some thirty yards away. It wasn't dead, but he was damned certain it soon would be. Forcing down the gear stick, he threw the bus into forward and stepped down hard on the accelerator pedal.

'*Help!* For the love of God, help me!' it cried.

Benford's hands tightened on the steering wheel as he aimed straight for it.

We do hope that you have enjoyed reading this large print book.

Did you know that all of our titles are available for purchase?

We publish a wide range of high quality large print books including:
Romances, Mysteries, Classics
General Fiction
Non Fiction and Westerns

Special interest titles available in large print are:
The Little Oxford Dictionary
Music Book, Song Book
Hymn Book, Service Book

Also available from us courtesy of Oxford University Press:
Young Readers' Dictionary
(large print edition)
Young Readers' Thesaurus
(large print edition)

For further information or a free brochure, please contact us at:
Ulverscroft Large Print Books Ltd.,
The Green, Bradgate Road, Anstey,
Leicester, LE7 7FU, England.
Tel: (00 44) 0116 236 4325
Fax: (00 44) 0116 234 0205

Other titles in the
Linford Mystery Library:

BLING-BLING, YOU'RE DEAD!

Geraldine Ryan

When the manager of newly-formed girl band Bling-Bling needs a Surveillance Operator to protect them, retired policeman Bill Muir jumps at the chance — but he doesn't know what he's let himself in for . . . In *Making Changes*, Tania Harkness is on a mission to turn around her run-down estate. But someone else is equally determined to stop her . . . And in *Another Country*, Shona Graham returns to her native Orkney island of Hundsay to put right a wrong that saw her brother ostracised by the community many years previously . . .

THE OTHER FRANK

Tony Gleeson

When Detective Frank Vandegraf hears of the unexpected death of his ex-wife, he travels to the tiny rural town of Easton to face the demons of his past. But it's no respite from the challenging urban crimes of his regular job. No sooner has he arrived than two bizarre, violent deaths occur, and he feels irresistibly drawn to help unravel a web of mystery and intrigue. However, he's out of his jurisdiction, obstructed by officials, and amidst folk hiding their own secrets . . .

THE DOPPELGÄNGER DEATHS

Edmund Glasby

While investigating a fatal car crash, Detective Inspector Vaughn's interest is piqued when forensic evidence points to murder, and he is shown the eerie antique doll found sitting on the passenger seat. The blood-spattered doll bears an extraordinary resemblance to the dead man, and on its lap is an envelope containing the message: 'One down. Five to go.' When a second doll is discovered beside another murder victim, the desperate race is then on to find and stop the killer from completing the set of six murders . . .